THE ARK

THE ARK

and Other Fantastic Tales

ANNA CATES

RESOURCE *Publications* • Eugene, Oregon

THE ARK
And Other Fantastic Tales

Resource Publications
An Imprint of Wipf and Stock Publishers
199 W. 8th Ave., Suite 3
Eugene, OR 97401

www.wipfandstock.com

PAPERBACK ISBN: 979-8-3852-3786-9
HARDCOVER ISBN: 979-8-3852-3787-6
EBOOK ISBN: 979-8-3852-3788-3

02/25/25

For Kason

Contents

Acknowledgments

"The Ark" first appeared in *Agape Review* on July 25, 2022.

The late Saundra M. Cates, my mother, was the primary author of "The Ark." After her death, I typed up the story from her journal, make minor edits, and added the ending before finding a suitable publisher in *Agape Review*.

"The Exorcism" first appeared in *Quail Bell* on September 15, 2023.

"Orc" first appeared as a prose poem in Abyss & Apex on April 1, 2021 and was later republished in *Little Black Box: Speculative Poetry from Ohio* (Wipf & Stock 2023).

Thanks to *The Writers of the Future Contest* for awarding honorable mention prizes to original versions of "The Exorcism" and "Flower Strong."

The Ark

Decades before it started to rain, our preparations began. You cannot imagine how fervently and relentlessly we worked. Always the dread of the unknown, impending disaster lurked in our consciousness to spur us onward lest we should waver in our tasks. We didn't know when it would happen or how long we would have to endure, only that each day was urgent, and there was no time for anything but work, work, work.

We didn't have many friends from the village. They found us strange, even dangerous, because of our beliefs. "Give it a rest, Noah," the nicest of them would say with a smirk. Father and Mother made it clear that we should have as little contact with the villagers as possible. People were cruel, violent, and quick to harm. It was not a happy way to grow up. It was downright scary! But at least we had each other. At least we didn't live in the city states, constantly at war.

As boys, we sometimes wished we could join in the hunting and sportsmanship, have time for fun or lazing about. But Father would get that stern look in his sad eyes, and we knew it was useless to even think about it. So, it was back to work.

The enormous structure we were building exhausted us. But we became experts in the timber business. We built wagons and sledges to carry the huge logs from the forest and perfected metal instruments for the cutting and tooling of great logs. We bought, taught, and trained animals for the job. We kept horses, oxen, and even some elephants for the heaviest work. They had to be housed and cared for every day.

Mother, too, had quite the daunting task of caring for animals. She tended cattle, goats, sheep, and chickens, plus many herding dogs that helped with the stock. She was very busy, and frequently children and young maidens from the village would come to work for her to help with the overwhelming tasks. It is a blessing from God that we were all such big, strong people! Mother also tended a vegetable garden and orchard. We shared delicious meals with our hired help. We did not eat meat like the villagers, but with fresh bread, milk and cheese, nuts, berries, and fruit, we were well nourished. Mother was also an expert in gathering and preparing wild plants for edibles and medicines, so we lacked for nothing. Even so, it was lonely sometimes.

Then, one day, we found Sophia. We were in the forest for another load of logs. We had heard a commotion earlier, coming from the rocky hillside, and so were watchful for trouble. Throughout the country, and beyond, roving bands of wild men trekked about, making all kinds of mischief, stealing, and destroying whatever, or whoever, they wanted. It was best to keep your senses sharp. Also, wolves and wild dogs roamed the mountains. We stayed armed and ready wherever we went.

The logging road wound through the forest, and as it came out of the trees, the rocky hillside trail led down to the valley. Looking back as we left the trees, the long afternoon shadows were already darkening the woods behind us, and the sun was low in the evening sky. It would never do to be out after dark in such times. That was when the predators, animal and human, emerged to do their ungodly deeds, so it was with some sense of urgency that we kept to the well-worn road as it led down to the village.

Then Father paused and motioned for us to stay still. He peered sideways through the trees at a large boulder. He called me to follow behind him as Ham and Japeth waited on the road. We drew closer. I could tell it was a naked body, stretched out motionless, face down. Father removed the coverlet from his shoulders and approached the still body. He averted his eyes and thew the blanket over the form and began tucking the cloth around the exposed skin. Already, though it was not yet dark, a chill had entered the air. Father bid me help him take the body off the rock. Even in the dimming light, I could see her face! She was a beautiful, young maiden, bruised, bleeding, and barely alive. Obviously, the victim of some heinous crime by the wild men, or maybe even some of the so-called monkey people who hadn't yet been slaughtered by the Nephilim who ruled the war-troubled city states. But I doubted such persons even existed anymore.

We carried the girl's limp body to the safety of the logs. I sat holding her head gently on my lap for the ride back. My brothers gathered round to see her face behind the wild mass of dark, tangled hair mixed with blood.

At last, Father drove the team into our barnyard. My brothers took care of the logs and saw to the animals as Father and I carried her in to Mother. Mother quickly directed us to place her in the spare room by the kitchen. She then gave orders to prepare hot water and bring the necessary herbs and ointments for the girl's care. After Mother had bathed and tended her, which took most of the evening, she told us our new guest was alive but very ill-used and still unconscious.

It was a somber supper that night as we gathered around the table for hot soup, cheese, and bread. Never had the wild men come so close to our home and the village. Father said soon it would not be safe to live here in the open anymore. Thankfully, since the ark was finished, we would start to move into its shelter as soon as God said it was time. We did not have long to wait.

The next week, when Father came from the prayer room, he announced that God had told him that it was time for us to move into the ark. Although we already stored many things there, we still would have much to do to finish the final preparations. Some of the stalls and feeding troughs needed finishing as well as our beds and storage bins. All furniture was made solid with the ark, so there would be no shifting during the storm we anticipated. We did not know how the animals would be brought, but Father said God would take care of that, which was always his answer, and he was always right.

Then the day came when Mother brought Sophia out to have supper with us. It was easy to see that she and Mother had forged a strong family bond. Sophia was lovely, and quiet, but she seemed happy. Mother told us that Sophia would be staying with us from now on. She had no family outside the ark, and her village was far away and would soon be covered with water in the flood. We were the only safety, security, and love she had ever known, or would know, so naturally she didn't want to leave. I was relieved to know that and had begun to believe that God had provided in Sophia a wife for me. There simply was no other answer. I was fearful that she might be frightened of all men after her horrible treatment by the wild men, so I was always very quiet and soft-spoken with her, as were we all.

One night, after our meal, I presented her with a beautiful necklace of emerald and pearl that I had made in our workshop. She smiled and seemed very pleased. I spoke to Father and Mother the next day so they could ask her to be my bride. They were glad that now all their sons had wives. My brothers had already found mates from the village girls who helped mother. Now if only my sweet Sophia would agree, we could all be as one. To my great joy, she said *yes*! The next day, Father married us before our evening meal. It was an especially sumptuous feast, with even some honey cakes for dessert! Father said we would move into the ark the following day.

Early in the morning, we awoke to animal sounds and ground shaking as animals in lines approached our ark. They seemed eager to board, but not unruly. We guided the larger animals in first after Mother and our wives had finished checking on the feeding stations to be sure all was prepared for the journey, however long it might be. God blessed the animals so that they came in orderly and quietly. They went straight to their piles of hay, and after eating, entered a peaceful sleep.

Dark skies and wild, unusual cloud formations grew even more ominous as evening approached and the last of the animals came. The top row of windows remained open, and birds came flying in all day like chickens arriving to roost before night. The darkness and coolness seemed to trigger a hibernation instinct among the creatures. God had prepared them to understand that they were in danger and that the ark was their only shelter for whatever was coming.

The people in the nearby villages up and down the river were not as aware as the animals. For years, curious ones had come to see the big boat under construction beyond Fara, the nearby village on a tributary leading into the Tigris-Euphrates River. Father always spoke to them in small groups, explaining that God had warned him of a great flood and to prepare for such a disaster. He said everything, all that had breath under Heaven, would die. Nothing and no one would be safe as even the mountains would sink beneath the waves. Most laughed at him. Some found him simply crazy. A hundred and twenty years passed. The few people that seemed to listen, at first, began to shake their heads, roll their eyes, and walk away.

The crowds became more hostile and abusive. They no longer listened as Father tried to reason with them. They shouted and waved their arms about. Some even threw rocks from their slings. They threatened even to tear down or burn all we had crafted, so we knew the time was near.

The last creatures came aboard. We finished loading our personal items we would need for the voyage into the unknown. Nothing would ever be the same. All would be changed. The beautiful river valley, our sunny hills, the colossal forest trees, and the majestic mountains would vanish! Everything not on board the ark would be swept away! It was too much to comprehend! We solemnly entered the big door with the last load. We carried the precious writings and artifacts from our holy forebears: Lamech, Enoch, even Adam and Eve, who walked and talked with God before he expelled them from Eden.

Sacred writings we'd preserved and packed in wrappings and water-proofed trunks. The sacred and priceless items were the heritage and core of who we hoped to become as a people. We had to save them for those who afterwards would repopulate the world. It was a grand and awesome assignment. We were honored to be chosen by God, but with trembling determination stepped forward into the next step of the perilous journey.

God closed the big door and sealed it behind us! We gathered inside with our arms around one another in prayer for God to protect us and save us in the coming storm.

A shutter blew open near to me. I peered outside into the dark downpour. Rain beat down hard as a waterfall. Yet even through the rain, I could see the comet tear across the sky—a harbinger of doom.

The pressure deepened, thick and heavy, descending. My ears popped painfully. The storm exploded with booming thunder and blinding flashes of lightening that continued for what seemed like forever. We went to our beds and huddled there beneath the soft, warm covers and continued to pray as the storm raged. Can you imagine multiple severe earthquakes, Tsunamis, and hurricanes happening all over the world all at the same time? We didn't have to imagine it. We lived through it!

Unfortunately, for everyone and everything outside the ark, it was a watery hell of no escaping! God's tender love sheltered only us. Under his mighty wings we remained so that we did not have to see or fully perceive the destruction going on all around us. Like little children, we snuggled close to Heavenly Father and trusted him to care for us. It was the only way!

Daily after that, Father would rise to light the oil lamps so we could move around, eat something, and check the cargo. The creatures were all sleeping, so there was not much to do. We returned to our beds. This routine continued for days, weeks, and months.

I can still remember the strange and uneasy sensation when the waters rose sufficiently to cause the ark to float. God had prepared us for this experience since we had been in and out of boats all our lives and were used to the constant rocking. Still, it was shockingly rough at first. By God's mercies, we did not get sick but grew accustomed to the continuous motion until it was an everyday reality.

Occasionally, Father climbed the long stairway to the top deck to see if the waters were abating. I only went up a few times. Sophia did not want me to be away from her, and I did not want to cause her added stress in her condition. (Yes, halleluiah! She became with child!) We were very happy and believed God would soon give us a sign that the waters were receding. We longed to feel the solid earth beneath our feet again!

But outside, it always looked the same. Water, water everywhere, and no land in any direction.

Toward the very end of our voyage, as we held our weekly prayer vigil, Sophia leapt to her feet, tilted her head toward Heaven, and began prophesying. She spoke of a future cataclysm of fire. She spoke of a holy one who would come before that time to save all the people from their sins and the powers of darkness. I trembled. Tears streamed down my cheeks as she spoke of this future savior as the new ark of salvation. At that moment, it occurred to me that, though God's wrath is severe and justified, his love is greater still, and he would make a way for all people to come to him, even those who didn't deserve his grace, people like the wild men, like the ones who laughed at us and threw rocks, even like those wicked people that hurt Sophia, those who were so hard to forgive. I was flooded with conviction that it all would come to pass.

The Exorcism

I n ancient days, a priestly order roamed the earth, some corrupt, others true . . .

The demon had disappeared! Dismayed, Chizedek scanned the ruins of Telith Harn. Megalithic pillars, erected by primeval forebears, jutted upward. Long ago warring tribes had vandalized the engraved images, seeking to replace an enemy's gods with their own. Local villagers called the place a haunt for unclean spirits. He'd hoped to find Pithon, the demon he'd cast out of the prostitute, skulking about the ruins. He'd bet such an accursed place would attract him. But it seemed he'd been wrong.

Druida, Chizedek's ward and apprentice, peered about the ruins. "Is he here," she asked, wide-eyed and wary.

"No, girl. He's proving elusive."

"I thought you knew where to find him."

"He's fled." Though an experienced exorcist, Chizedek had allowed Pithon to outsmart him. He ground his teeth in frustrated rage at the mistake he'd made in casting out a demon without clarifying where it should go. "Go now to The Pit," he'd needed to add at the end of the exorcism, *before* Pithon tore out of the prostitute's mouth like a cloud of putrid darkness and escaped. The vile serpent had laughed, licked

Chizedek's face with a fiery tongue, then whorled away like a whirlwind, vanishing into dead air.

"Where will he go?" Druida asked. "What'll he do now?"

"Wander recklessly, seeking a new host to victimize, to empower and control for sordid purposes. If he finds entry into a prominent person, he could destroy the whole world!" Grimacing, Chizedek touched his cheek, seared and still pulsing with pain from the devil's tongue.

"Does it hurt?"

"Like Hell."

The relentless summer heat beat down. Chizedek wiped the sweat from his brow and removed the water bottle from the leather belt girding his robe. He gulped down several swigs of tepid water before offering Druida a drink. She lifted the bottle to her lips, swallowed, then handed it back to him.

"Can we return to the village now?" she asked.

"Not yet . . . " Chizedek was peering at the ground to his right. A peculiar pattern emerged in the sand that he hadn't noticed before. Snake tracks vacillated around a pillar then continued into the desert. "I found his trail! He's out there!" He pointed ahead into the sandy wasteland.

"How do you know that? How can you tell?" Druida's brow furrowed with incomprehension.

Chizedek pointed at the pattern. "The snake's tracks wind around the pillars then disappear into the brittlebushes and beyond."

"I see nothing!" Druida flailed her arms with vexation.

"Someday, child, you will see. Your discernment will grow. But you still have much to learn. Come. Follow me. We must find Pithon and banish him to The Pit, and I'll need you to help me."

"But the desert is full of the bones of foolish travelers, and sands that will swallow you alive. I don't want to die like that!"

"Be brave. Be strong. I need you."

"What for?" She stuck out her chin, standing resolute in her sandals and linen tunic.

"It takes two, at least."

"Why me?"

"You're all I have. Now come. Follow me." Chizedek grasped his staff and headed in the direction of the tracks.

"Wait! We did our best, Uncle Pa. Why can't we just let him go?" Druida called after him.

"We're not finished yet. Hurry along."

"Why couldn't you just leave that old woman alone? Why did you have to help her?"

"You don't mean that, girl."

"She was just some old whore."

"Every person matters to The Highest." Chizedek peered back, lips stiff. "Shall I leave you alone among the ruins for whatever rabble happens along, or will you stay with me and keep to The Way."

Druida's eyes rolled. Her hands fisted. She growled at the heavens then marched forward. "I'm coming! I'm coming!"

"Good." Following the snake tracks, Chizedek left Telith Harn and entered the desert, Druida lumbering along behind.

The subtle tracks whispered like wind, barely audible. They wound around the prickly pear and barrel cacti. They disrupted the paw prints of a sand cat. They crossed the silent steps of a desert mouse beside clumps of lonely ray flowers.

All was quiet in the desert but for the gentle hiss that called to him. Chizedek followed. A smoky charcoal scent lingered in the air, like brimstone, like incense . . . He remembered the prostitute, Nagwa. He'd found her at the village marketplace, loitering in alley shadows near the fig peddler's tent. The amulet she wore betrayed her profession, its emblem of the sun, broken lines swirling. She'd smiled at him. He'd first see the demon peering into her kohl-accented eyes, the black liner caked into wrinkles. She retained vestiges of youthful beauty, like a piece of fruit past its peak of ripeness, shriveled, but promising even greater sweetness, as grapes dry into raisins. Magnificent rugs and colorful pillows adorned her adobe abode on the outskirts of town in mountain shadow. She accepted only gold and silver. Fragrant oils perfumed her body, but her words were dry as the desert. She told him she was a pro, and he hadn't doubted it . . .

The snake tracks continued under clusters of sickly palms. Chizedek knew better than to trespass into the distant dunes. But a strange dizziness had entered his mind. His brain buzzed like a beehive. Despite the glaring sun, a darkness seemed to shroud him, the spiritual heaviness of the burden he bore. They passed a pile of bones.

"We shouldn't have come here," Druida said.

"Don't touch it."

"As if I would!"

Swirl, swirl, swirl . . . in the same redundant pattern, the snake tracks continued. Clusters of tumbleweed rolled aimlessly, broken twigs coiling and twirling like that symbol of the sun. He took one step then another. The pain in his cheek was numbing. He almost enjoyed the pain. He could train himself to like it if he tried hard enough . . .

"How much longer, Uncle Pa? You don't expect us to camp out here, do you?"

"Just a little farther. We're gaining on him," Chizedek said, though his bewilderment was growing. "Watch for signs and learn."

The sun was waning in the sky when he stopped in the path of a giant gazelle. Obsidian eyes stared at him. Sharp horns towered skyward. Air rushed through flaring nostrils. The gazelle wouldn't budge. The omen confused him. All he knew was they could go no further in that direction. He swung left, the tracks reappearing.

"This had better be the wonderful learning experience you keep promising," Druida lamented from behind. "You always castigate me to learn, learn, learn, but you never give me a chance to practice what I already know."

"Patience, girl. You'll have ample opportunity to practice before this day is through!" He peered back, surprised at his own words, but Druida wasn't listening. She didn't realize the difficulty he faced, the infection to his cheek. She was still a child, at least partly.

The sun hung low on the horizon as they ascended a small climb and came to a familiar sight: Telith Harn. Monolithic rocks cast long shadows across the sandy ground, littered with broken pebbles. The snake tracks led straight up to the biggest boulder. Pithon had outsmarted him again, led him in circles, mocking him, making a fool of him. Telith Harn *was* the demonic hangout after all.

"We're right back right where we started." Druida huffed. "Now what?"

"Silence, girl!" Chizedek said with a growl. "Listen! Pay attention. He's here! And it takes two."

"Why do you doubt me?"

They entered the stone circle. A woman's husky laughter sounded from some hidden place. Druida gasped. The hair stood up on Chizedek's neck. A chorus of hissing, like multiple voices, reverberated in his ears. Pithon was no longer in solo! Chizedek no longer faced a single foe! He peered left then right. "Show yourself! In the name of The One True God, I command you to manifest!"

"It takes two," Druida whispered, standing nearby, alert now and ready to assist.

"What it takes, you don't have." Nagwa stepped out from behind a pillar, dressed in red silk. Her kohl-accented eyes flittered between them with lack of appreciation. She wore a king cobra across her shoulders like a hyperborean queen her luxurious furs. She flaunted it. Wrinkled cleavage cradled her amulet. "But I won't hold that against you." Her henna-painted lips curled into a smirk. Legions of laughter reverberated from her throat before another shadow jumped off a pillar and entered her through her mouth. She rocked back, absorbing the impact.

"Picked up a few friends along your travels, have you, Pithon?" Chizedek said to Nagwa.

"I've missed you, my pet," Nagwa purred, her voice mixing with other voices not her own. "Come back to my bed. We had a good time, you and I."

"Heavenly Father, protect us . . . " Druida prayed.

"Shut up!" said Pithon and his Legion, moving Nagwa's lips like a puppeteer.

"Who's in there?" Chizedek asked Nagwa.

"Believe in me, and I will show you," Nagwa replied. "You will see us shining like polished bronze, covered in gems! You will see The Magnificent Morning Star!"

"You're a liar!" Druida said. "You're fallen and dim."

"In the name of The King of Heaven, I command you to tell us who you are!" Chizedek said.

Nagwa grinned devilishly. "I am Lord of Fear, risen from the ashes!"

"Lord of Fear?" Chizedek nodded. "I've heard of you. Who else abides within you?"

Nagwa threw back her arms, assuming another guise. "I am The Great God of The Desert Mountains!"

"I know your ilk. Who else residences in Nagwa's body?" Chizedek continued with command. "Who is the strong man among you?"

Nagwa ducked her head with cunning. "The Many-Faced One who rules in The Place of Silence." Hissing filled the air. Fire shrouded Nagwa.

"I bind you together, fiery serpents!" Chizedek swirled his staff through the air in a circular motion as if wrapping Legion with a chord.

"No!" Nagwa clawed at her flesh, leaving bloody scratches. "I will not be bound!"

"Monster, lie down!" Druida said. "Glide away. Return to the ashes!"

"No, I will shed my skin and renew myself!"

"Fall down," Chizedek said, as if training a dog obedience, pointing to the earth with his staff. "Crawl away! Eat the dust!"

Nagwa roared with rage. "I don't have to listen to you!"

"Nagwa," he said. "You must resist the spirits."

Druida nodded. "Resist them!"

"Remove the amulet," Chizedek said.

"Take it off." Druida nodded.

Nagwa's eyes flooded with confusion. Some part of her wanted deliverance. Her hand rose. She touched the sun symbol. But Legion was so powerful, so many. Her hand returned to her side, and her confused expression faded into new resolve. "Revere me, and I will reward you, give you earthly treasure, anything you desire!"

Chizedek shook his head. "You are accursed and have nothing to give but curses."

"No, you're wrong," Nagwa said. "We can empower you, help you to do good. Let us in!"

"You have been cast down," Druida said.

"Let us in! Let us in!" Voices hissed in the dark, wind whipping up little maelstroms of sandy particles.

"Crawl away to The House of Dust, Serpent of The Underworld!" Chizedek swept his staff through the air.

"I hate you!" Empowered by Legion, Nagwa rushed forward to attack him.

"Beast, lie down!" Chizedek knocked her aside with the staff.

Nagwa toppled to the earth, skidding over pebbles, only to rise back up, glowering. "I will destroy you!" She lunged at him again, haloed all in hisses.

"Turn over! Glide into the ground!" He struck her with the staff, propelling her against towering rock. Her eyes glassed over then refocused, crazed. "Let your two poison glands be in the ground." Chizedek maneuvered his staff, readying for the next attack. "Spittle in the dust!"

Nagwa trembled. Shadows danced about her. "I will enter you!" Dark lightning burst from her mouth, catching Chizedek off guard. He lifted his staff, but the demon knocked into him before he could speak. The staff flew out of his grasp. He fell to the ground. The demon leapt onto him. Fangs tore into his shoulder. The pain was searing. He yowled in agony, the wound steaming.

"Heavenly Father, help us!" Druida cried, grabbing the staff.

"Holy One . . . " Chizedek said through gritted teeth, crushed beneath the demon's weight. Jaws like meat hooks snagged and ripped his tortured flesh. "Holy One . . . Druida!"

"Holy Father, help us!" Druida prayed. "Send your clean spirit servants!"

Liquid lightning flashed down, then another. Druida pointed the staff at the demon upon him. "In the name of The Highest King of Heaven, I bind you and rebuke you and send you now to The Pit!"

Fire erupted from the staff, covering Chizedek . . . holy, healing fire. The demon shrieked and let go. It fled back into Nagwa's mouth, but the flames followed. The conflagration engulfed her. She staggered to-and-fro then sank to her knees, toppled over, and balled up into a fetal position, shivering.

Druida rushed to her side. "Are you okay?" she asked, stooping over her.

"They've left me!" Nagwa spoke in a whisper. "I wanted freedom for so long. Thank you!"

The world stilled. Chizedek lay on his back on the earth. The constellations flickered above him, signs and seasons glinting, imparting peace. "Is she alive?" he asked.

"She didn't make it," Druida said, walking back to him solemnly with the staff. "All those demons were just too much for her, poor soul." She stood over him with newfound poise, seeming unusually adept. "Now I understand what happened."

"You do?"

"You lied to me."

"I did?"

"You didn't visit her to help her. You went to 'help yourself.' For favors."

"I *had* planned to help her!" Chizedek clenched his fist. "I just fell short of my good intentions. But you're right. I've lied to you, myself, and Heavenly Father. I compromised myself with her. That's why only you could complete the exorcism. I told you I needed you."

Druida nodded. "I understand now why it takes two. Where one is weak, another is strong. But how could you get so off-centered? Your straying from The Way could have killed us both!"

"I'm not perfect, Druida. My mind strayed, just for a moment, into an unspiritual way of thinking, and I fell."

Druida pursed her lips with a huff. She placed one hand on her hip, tapping her toes on the dusty ground. "At least the demons are gone." She stretched out her hand. "Let me help you back up."

Chizedek smiled, taking her hand. "You've learned more than I thought. I'm proud of you."

The Star Child

They had to leave, flee their land, seek new horizons, hope in fate, in divine providence, risk everything, brave every danger, stumble forward in the dark, over seas, under stars, or through stars to new shores . . .

Constance Mather stepped through the brush, positioning her boot so the raspberry thorns wouldn't tear her brown linen skirt. Sweet and juicy, the berries had ripened to perfection. She popped a corpulent morsel onto her eager tongue, not forbidding herself the pleasure. Sleeves rolled up, forearms lightly scratched from briars, she leaned forward, stretching stained fingers for another cluster. She looked forward to pie and appreciated an excuse to get away from her stepmother, Sarah, who was difficult to please, prim and exacting.

Sarah, her father's new lawful wife, could never take the place of her mother, whose death due to the travails of childbirth had left a hollow ache in her soul. Yet Constance felt the need to withstand Sarah, if only for her father's sake, difficult though that was. Before he exited the cabin each morning for his daily burden, her father bestowed upon this new woman, barely more than a stranger, the same noisy kiss on the cheek as he had to her mother. Constance could hardly stand it.

Sarah believed that hard work, an ardent refraining from idleness, would wean Constance from her grief. Thin-lipped and flush-cheeked, this new mother, grafted awkwardly into her life, sought every opportunity to righten her. She harbored the suspicion that wayward girls from their community—she knew not who—had been in secret "dancing with the devil" in the woods. She'd warned Constance about the consequences of such folly. How hot were those fires of Hell! "Witchcraft and devilry manifest in many guises," Sarah had cautioned her. The thought of such terrors bewildered and horrified Constance.

Yet despite her piety, at times Sarah made Constance feel as if she were secretly laughing at her and their whole Puritan community, making Constance question the depth of Sarah's sincerity. Between the cracks in her strictures, there seemed to ooze out profound doubts, silently broadcast in facial expressions, scowls and smirks. Yet, for the good or for the bad, Constance had to accept her father's sudden inclination for the "buxom work horse," to use her older brother's terms.

In ferreting out a new clump of bushes, Constance arrived at a section of forest with broken and toppled trees. Circular scorch marks had burned into the underbrush. She froze, puzzled and alarmed. Could Sarah be right? Had someone been "dancing with the devil" in the woods, leaving in nature a visible wound? Constance forced the thought from her mind. It must be the work of passing settlers, newcomers her father warned her they must avoid. Baptists, Anglicans, Lutherans, and the like were not Puritans. Hordes upon hordes of trespassers, though professing Christ, were still corrupted by the world. Constance shuddered at the thought of their deception, considering her own salvation spider web thin and porous, tenuous from the taint of Original Sin.

She passed through the wounded woods and arrived at the Winthrop homestead, burned to the ground five years prior. Only the rock foundation remained. The conflagration had consumed both the structure and the whole Winthrop family. Constance shuddered at the thought of death by fire. How horrible to die like a witch, screaming and melting like tallow amid black brimstone. She wondered why God had allowed such a tragedy and if the Winthrops had done something to deserve it.

She considered exploring the lonely ruins but thought better of it. Walking around the perimeter of the weedy acreage, she came to a mandrake patch, confronted by the large glossy leaves and poison berries, crimson as sin. A Winthrop must have planted it. Who else could be responsible? Unlike tobacco, Indians didn't use the twisted little man, forked as a bifurcated mind, who, if pulled up from the roots by the hair of his head, would emerge from loose loam screaming like a demon before an exorcist's cross. He was no innocent, no corncob doll. He came in every aberrant form, his face pale and frozen like the man in the moon, tapering legs twisting together like a sailor's knot, unpartable, or spread eagle and curlicued as a fiddlehead, seeming ready for a wispy toe dance. Constance wished he were only a plant. But mandrake was more than that, an omen, boding nebulous portends.

As she moved on, a soft ball of light floated over the treetops. Then it disappeared. Constance gasped. She wondered if it might be a "wonder in the heavens" spoken of in scripture, a sign from God.

God. His name was Jealous. Jealous with a capital J! She knew better than to spite him. She didn't think she had. Could it be that she was special that he would gift her with a sign? If so, she could never tell anyone. How arrogant that would sound. She shuddered at the thought. Besides, nobody would believe her. Her paternal grandfather had called her a "silly goose" with a "head full of fancies and fiddlesticks." Perhaps her mind was just playing tricks on her. "I mustn't drift into idle thoughts," Constance whispered to herself, forced the ball of light from her mind, and hastened to add more raspberries to her pail.

That summer day, the Massachusetts Bay Colony had settled into a languid warmth, provoking a bit of dew about her brow, yet with ocean breezes moderating. A soft buzzing sounded in her ears, but she saw no bees. The buzzing continued, so peculiar. It seemed a mystery. "This new world is so strange," Constance said.

Her diligence with the berries continued until the sun was sinking in the sky and her pail nearly spilling over, the handle's hinge creaking as it swayed. Constance stepped away from the bushes, ready to return home.

She scanned the forest's edge, trying to determine where she'd exited the wilderness for the clearing. She spotted two familiar trees, a pine and a maple, and proceeded through the tall grasses toward them, pail groaning in her grasp. Again, that soft buzzing thudded in her ears, followed her steps.

Constance felt as if someone were watching her. She peered left then right but discerned no one. She and her family lived furthest from the village, with no close neighbors since the Winthrops' demise, so she couldn't imagine who it might be. She was certain enough no Indians were near. They had moved further inland. She had no knowledge of hermits, witches, or other outcasts, abiding alone in the woods. Might she be intruding upon fairies or elves unawares? The thought of such magical creatures remedied her concerns. And did she not have a guardian angel to protect her?

The faint buzzing thudded again, pulsing in her ears. A strange sensation tingled through her. Relaxation, an unusual peace, tranquilized like sleep. She wanted to sit down for a moment and contemplate life's mysteries and couldn't help but note an attractive patch of matted Indian grass beneath a tulip tree where she could do so.

She set her pail on the grass then sat down near to it, half in shade, half in light. Leaves rustled with the breeze, a red-winged blackbird lending to the day its conk-la-ree. She leaned back against the bark with a sigh, arms around her knees, letting the mild sweet scent of the yellow-green and orange tulip tree blossoms lull her senses. Daylight would soon end and the cloudless blue darken and flood with constellations while the hoot owls yoo-hooed . . .

She'd seen a shooting star, sizzling across the canopy of night, and it had filled her with wonder. She'd seen a day moon, so full, pink and swollen, it hung low as summer's fruit over the duckpond's reflective mirk, and it had stirred within her such longing. She'd thought how sweet it would be, Puritan or not, to shed every garment and run feral as a dam through raw wilderness . . .

The Star Child came so quietly, so gently, it caused no arrest. Half dreaming, half awake, Constance felt its presence draw near. Its unearthly charisma filled her with calm. A long luminous finger stroked her cheek. The bulbous tip touched the rim of her collar, studied a loose brown lock, escaping her bonnet that soon slipped off her head.

She looked into its eyes. Friendship. Fascination. Something like love, or at least respect, intelligence perceiving she was wonderfully human, not merely a girl, but as wonderfully human as any man or woman, settler or Indian. Strange worlds and wonders gleamed in the mesmerizing opals. The swollen head should have seemed odd, but she could tell all was as it should be. She didn't even notice that her bodice had loosened . . .

When Constance arrived back at the cabin, the crickets were singing and the first stars glinting. She crept through the door and quietly placed her bucket on the wooden table. Her father and brother, helping an injured congregant tend his farm, at Sarah's insistence, would be late in getting home.

Sarah sped around from the countertop where she was butchering a cod, a fishy scent wafting about her solid frame. "Where have you been?" she rasped, face flushed, bun tight, minus a few wisps.

"I've brought berries, Ma'am, for pie." Constance gestured toward her pickings.

Sarah set down the filleting knife and wiped her wet hands on her apron. "The garden is full of weeds, and you've been gone all day! It's dark outside. Coming home after dusk is not decent for a young lady!"

Constance ducked her head. She knew that was true. "There were just so many berries, Ma'am. I wouldn't they be wasted."

"Not decent!" Sarah repeated as if Constance hadn't heard or understood. She paced. "Your bonnet is off your head!"

"It was windy." Constance shrugged, with stained fingers, fidgeting with the ties of her bonnet that lay loosely over her two rumpled braids.

"And your lace isn't straight, not that you should wear anything so fancy at all."

"I didn't realize it was showing." Constance tucked it down and away from sight.

"Perhaps you were more than just berry-picking." Sarah's dark eyes gleamed with mistrust. "Did you meet someone in the woods?"

Constance gasped. "No, ma'am! That would be unseemly!"

"An Indian boy?"

Constance huffed. "No, ma'am. Nobody!"

"A Quaker?"

"I saw the Anderson twins throwing rotten vegetables at them on their way out of town, but I've never spoken to any of them. Ever!"

Sarah's eyes narrowed. "You're hiding something. You're lying to me. Perhaps I should search your pockets for witch's herbs."

Constance turned her skirt pockets inside out. "My pockets are empty, Ma'am, except for . . . Whoops." Puzzling, she held up between two stained fingers a piece of twisted root, dumbfounded as to its origins.

"Mandrake!" Sarah gasped.

"I don't know how that got in my pocket!" Constance placed it on the table, quickly retracting her hand as if the chunk were burning hot.

"It's you. You're one of them. You've been dancing with the devil in the woods!"

Constance flailed her arms. "They're not devils! They're not from here. I can't explain. You wouldn't understand."

Sarah shrieked and clawed the air. "Oh, you wicked child! I knew this would happen. Oh, I knew it when I saw that ugly brown witch's mark on your shoulder!"

"You're not my mother! And yes, I've been dancing with the devil in the woods! And I didn't just dance. I sang too! I danced and sang in my fancy lace till the sun turned black and bowed down to the moon!"

The open palm landed with a sting against Constance's cheek. She reeled a step backward at the impact.

"Not in this house, young lady!" Sarah said.

"I hate you! I hate You!" Constance grabbed a fistful of berries from the bucket and threw them at Sarah, who screeched as the soggy bits pelted her.

"You're not my mother!" Constance sped out the door and ran through the fallow field toward the woods, flashing with fireflies, ameliorating the darkness, a full moon hovering like a ghost over the treetops.

"Come back here, wicked girl! Where do you think you're going?" Sarah cried. Then she exploded into crazy laughter. "If you find him, save some for me!"

It occurred to Constance that Sarah was a "double-minded woman," as their minister would say, and had placed the mandrake in her pocket herself. How else could it have gotten there? She had rooted up like a wild boar, from God-cursed earth, the forked vegetable man and chopped him into pieces for magical rite, relegating fragments of intended effect however she saw fit.

Ignoring Sarah's cries, Constance continued toward the little trail through the woods, choking on the sobs engulfing her. "Star Child! Come back! Take me with you!"

She could never be a good Puritan again. She had changed, and the community would never understand . . .

In the days that followed, the villagers searched and searched for Constance, but all was vanity. Yet one of the Taylor boys found her bonnet, strangely, hanging from the topmost branch of a giant spruce, near the cliffs, overlooking the restless sea.

Flower Strong

I

The time comes in every king's life when knights and bodyguards won't suffice. Some tasks require an assassin.

King Alvon turned to the shifty-eyed man in worn leather. "I hear you're a man of discretion."

A sly grin, a slight bow. "Balfor of Blackbridge at your service." He spoke with a lisp. "What's your want?"

"A take down."

"My specialty. Who?"

"Flower Strong."

Balfor's brows rose. "That orc wench taking sanctuary here? The one your son spends all his time with?"

Annoyed at the observation, King Alvon toyed with his wine goblet before setting it back on the table by the window overlooking the lake. "Aye. Flower Strong. She's an impediment to my purposes. You needn't know more."

Balfor's scent of sweat and cheap cologne filled the room. "May I sport with her first?"

King Alvon rolled his eyes. "Dispose of her however you please. Play your cat and mouse game. Just make sure you finish her off."

"How much?"

"A pouch of silver."

Balfor sneered. "I want gold!"

A weak laugh escaped King Alvon's mouth. "You'd never get away with gold. It would arouse suspicions. You're too lowborn." King Alvon scanned Balfor disdainfully. "Silver is as good as you can do."

Balfor shrugged. "Then I'll settle for silver. When?"

"Tonight, after the banquet. Flower Strong shelters in the cottage behind the castle, near the chicken coop, where she tends the hens. The gate will be unlocked. And don't forget; the penalty for betrayal is worse than death." He waved two fingers through the air dismissively.

"Your Grace." Balfor bowed then exited the room.

No sooner had King Alvon regained his solitude than a knock sounded at the door. "Come in," he said, knowing only someone he might wish to see would dare approach him.

Gordan, his nineteen-year-old son, and Ariel, the weird woman, entered.

"Who was that lout?" Gordan asked. "And why do you accept such company?"

King Alvon laughed darkly. "You're one to talk, considering the company you've been keeping. But to answer your question, he's just some rogue from Blackbridge I've hired to spy on our guests, just until the conference ends. Stay out of his way, and his business."

"Whatever!" Gordan smirked, projecting his distempered mood.

Ariel stepped forward in her silvery tunic, black boots clicking across the floor. "Your Grace, I've introduced Gordan to Princess Felicity. There seems to be an understanding. By the end of the conference, their betrothal should be official." She clapped her hands together silently as if the arrangement were snug as pat.

"I won't marry Felicity, Father," Gordan said.

"Oh, yes, you will," King Alvon replied.

"My heart is not at liberty, Father."

"You will do your duty and marry her," King Alvon said.

"I won't!"

Ariel pursed her lips. "I *must* agree with your father, Gordan, for the sake of the alliance, for the sake of peace."

Gordon flailed his arms. "Butt out, you meddlesome hag! This doesn't concern you!"

Ariel's dark eyes flickered with ire, but she steadied herself, striving for dignity. "Every matter of state concerns me. I realize you're lovesick, Gordan, but you mustn't speak to me that way. I am a faithful public servant, advisor to His Highness, and your onetime tutor."

"We should have thrown you in the fire ages ago, you worthless witch!" Gordan said. "This whole marriage scheme was your idea! This is your fault!"

"Silence!" King Alvon lifted his fist. "Ariel, leave us."

Ariel paused, forehead creased with consternation, then turned for the door. She peered back but once, angry eyes flashing, then exited with a huff. The wooden door fell back into place, sealing monarch and son into their fate.

King Alvon paced to the window, peered out at the lake and forested hills, then turned back to address his son. "Princess Felicity is not without her charms, a respectable four years your senior, virtuous, if a bit stiff, but a perfect match; you must agree."

"Aye. She is, for someone, but not for me. Father, I've decided not to marry. I will sire heirs through concubinage only."

The king's head rocked back with a laugh. "It's been one hundred years since our house practiced concubinage. It's an old, forgotten way."

"It's my legal right. I'll press the matter with council if I must."

"You'd get nowhere."

"You'd be surprised how far I'd get."

"And what's that supposed to mean?"

Gordan shrugged, self-assured. "I've already drawn up a contract."

"And I suppose Flower Strong will be your designated consort?"

Gordan grinned. "My one and only. I can't thank you enough, Father, for granting her clemency."

"A mistake I've since regretted."

"She's not like the other orcs, Father. She's clean and healthy, not deformed by disease and devil worship."

"A half-orc cannot be your heir!"

"Flower Strong is good, purified by sacred fire."

"She's an *orc*, Gordan! She has fangs!"

"So what? So does your cat, Miss Prissy! Flower Strong's are tiny! She's beautiful!"

"She's a beast!" King Alvon wanted to add "ripe for slaughter," but thought better of it.

"She makes me happy, and I am resolved."

"Marrying Felicity is your responsibility. And you'll do it!" King Alvon turned away. Gordan's obstinance would have enraged him even more, but Flower Strong would soon be dead and his foolish son heartbroken. Anxiety, more than ire, filled him lest his scheme should fail. To have blood on your hands, even a monster's, was a worrisome affair. "We'll conclude this conversation later. Go!" He gestured toward the door. "Get ready for the banquet."

II

Torches glowed like the eyes of night along the walls of the banquet hall, and a wrought-iron chandelier hissed with candles. Waited on by attendants, nobles lined the tables, their greasy fingers stuffing delicacies into their mouths amid the chatter.

Seated in a corner, a bard with lute sang a festive tune about a wayward shepherdess. Across from him, a juggler in a page-boy haircut tossed up golden balls, at one moment, nearly crashing into a scullery maid, bringing braised carrots to the table. Ariel, wand in hand, incanted cryptic spells, strewing candy-colored smoke around the room to the amazement of all, the smoke curling into curious, bewildering images.

The wine flowed abundantly. King Alvon, though fearing he'd drunk too much already, raised his goblet and downed another swig of sparkly. The wild boar remained half-eaten, one side only ribs, the red delicious still intact. The king's burning eyes fixated on the tusks. Flower Strong's fangs curled up from her lower jaw in a similar fashion, though, indeed, they were tiny by comparison. Tipsy, he chuckled to himself, steaming like a demon, for there she was: Flower Strong, ladling stewed apricots onto the plate of some dandy from the House of Soloster, who bore a striking resemblance to Princess Felicity. The king's smoke-stung eyes swam from the princess to Flower Strong. Amazingly, even with her fangs, though in a tough, more muscular way, she seemed as becoming as the auburn-haired, sun-kissed princess, or maybe the wine was having its way with him.

At the sight of Flower Strong, taking up an empty platter, a lady in scarlet swooned against her escort, accidentally toppling to the floor her horns and gossamer headdress, exposing her bald spot.

The king winced. Allowing the notable time to reassemble herself and salvage her dignity, he sprang from his seat with raised goblet.

"Friends and soon-to-be family!" He held his cup forward. "I propose a toast: to the end of the Ten Year's War and the union of our kingdoms! May there be ten times ten years of blessings!"

"One hundred years of blessings, with peace and prosperity for all," Princess Felicity said, lifting her goblet along with her entourage.

On the other side of the room, furthest away from the princess, where he had not been bidden to sit, Prince Gordan sulked like a petulant child, picking at his venison and parsnips with lack of appreciation, absent-mindedly smashing green grapes with a silver spoon. Yet he perked visibly when Flower Strong neared him. *All too eager for her apricots*; the king noted bitterly. Teeth clenched, he blazed inside with unholy fire. *She'd make a good whore, for lesser men, but not my son.*

Gordan rose to his feet. "Lords and ladies, may I have your attention?"

A hush swept through the room. Flower Strong, in a cleavage-compressing corset and rustling skirt, stepped aside to give Gordan sway, her glistening curls bouncing. Yet he grabbed her by the arm, pulling her back, her apple blossom cheeks flushed with abashment. She managed to get the bowl of juicy fruit onto the table, with minimal spillage, just in time.

"Behold: a newcomer in our midst!" Gordan swept his hand through the air like a showman.

"Please, don't, Gordan," Flower Strong whispered, but the prince was glowing.

The king groaned with dismay, cupping his receding hairline. He shrank back into the hollow of his seat, his apprehension growing, unsure how best to handle the situation.

"Her name is Flower Strong," Gordan continued. "She hails from the orc-dom over the hills, yet she is no ordinary orc, is she? Neither is she a charlatan sorceress like our Lady Ariel," Gordan snorted as if he'd burgeoned a bull orc's pig snout himself. "She has been liberated from the evil powers that bound and ruined her breed! She has pilgrimaged down hallowed roads! She has passed through sacred fire and been cleansed! Divine Mystery has freed her! Let her be a lesson to us all!"

Several ladies gasped, while a tipsy baron cheered. "Show is a sign!" he said.

"Yes, dazzle us with your magic, if that be true," said the escort of the lady in the horned headdress.

"Prove it!" a voice cried.

"Show us," Felicity said. "If you are, indeed, a ransomed specimen, cast a spell."

"Show us! Show us!" the chant began. "Show us! Show us!" the aristocrats demanded in unison. They picked up their long pointy forks and knives like little devils and banged the handle ends on the table as they chanted. "Show us! Show us!" They chanted and laughed.

"Enough! Enough!" Prince Gordan cried, hushing the room. "Flower Strong, they have challenged you." Pulling her by the hand, he led her through an opening between two tables, arranged in a rectangle, and gained the room's center, only to step back, leaving Flower Strong the sole focal point.

The king sat frozen to his seat. He didn't want to openly rebuke his son in front of their guests, worsen the scene, and ruin the evening. He clenched his teeth, enduring the spectacle for the moment. *Flower Strong will be dead soon*, he assured himself. His eyes darting about the room, he lifted his wine cup with a shrug, trying to blame the grapes.

"Show them that you can do more than sew slippers, count eggs, and stew prunes," Prince Gordan said.

The king hunched forward on the pew, just curious enough to forbear his son to continue. What might Flower Strong present? A trick of the eye? A slight of the hand? Divine energy, if more than figment and fable, wouldn't commune with her ilk. Orc society respected nothing but pleasure and strength, at best. Yet she *was* different, and he *had* heard rumors of orc betterment, of light surpassing darkness, making redemption possible for all creatures made of flesh.

Flower Strong nodded at Prince Gordan then bowed her head as if in prayer or meditation. She held both hands forward, palms toward the ceiling. Then blue flame erupted from her fingertips.

The king gasped, as did Ariel, Felicity, and others. The lady in the horned headdress screamed then fainted in her seat.

The fire spread throughout the room yet burned no one, at least not physically. Yet before the conflagration could engulf him, King Alvon sprang from his seat and fled the hall, terrified and enraged.

III

Two hours after the midnight bell, the feasting had long since expired, and a stillness, like the shifting fog, had crept over the castle grounds. Riddled with misgivings, King Alvon paced alone in his bedchamber. He sensed some important piece of a puzzle was missing, and that frustrated him immensely. He wanted some glorious revelation to fall upon him like cleansing showers on a dry and dying land. In the absence of that, he reviewed the basic facts. Flower Strong could harness magic fire, a miraculous feat. She strove with esoteric powers, possessed mysterious spiritual aptitudes. She was dangerous. Amazingly so. Such technicalities hadn't factored into his decision to arrange for her death. Now he feared he'd acted too hastily. Killing her might be accursed, prone to backfire. Might there be another way? Was it too late? He stopped pacing as an idea came to him. If he stole down to the back of the castle, he might waylay the assassin and dismiss him from the task. But was it too late?

He dove for the closet and snatched his black cloak. The dark color and hood would conceal him in the shadows. Habitually, he affixed his sword to his belt.

He hastened from the room and hurried down the corridor to the spiral staircase. He descended as fast as he could without losing his footing on the narrow steps. He reached ground level and the arched opening, leading to secluded backyards. Brick walls and a wrought iron fence enclosed a poorly tended garden, as rank with weeds as florets and fruit trees. A hush hung over the orchard—the hens all slaughtered for the feast.

Heart thudding with dread at the bloody deed he might behold, the king slipped through the trees. He found a trail through the bramble, leading to the cottage and empty coop, overtaken by thorny vines with succulent blooms so aromatic they stung the senses.

A shadow slipped down a brick wall and thudded to the earth. The king turned. Though clouds partially covered the full moon, he discerned a figure in the gloom. *The cutthroat!* He hurried forward to catch him before he could strike. But to save his life, he couldn't remember the dirty bandit's name!

"You, there! Spppt," the king hissed.

"Halt!" a familiar voice returned.

"What? You? What are you doing here, prowling about the garden?" the king asked, removing his hood and letting down his guard, for there stood Gordan.

"I already know why you're here," Gordan said contemptuously. "Looking for your friend?"

"I don't have a friend—I . . . what do you mean?"

"That so-called spy you hired to kill Flower Strong. He slipped through the cottage window, not expecting to find *me* there with her. But I managed to get some answers out of him before I finished him off in the scuffle."

The king's mouth fell open with horror. "You mongrel! You've been porking her!"

Gordan withdrew his rapier. "Try to come between us again, snake! I *will* defend her! You'll taste my blade just like your cutthroat cohort!"

The king's head was spinning. He'd never thought of his son as a crazed killer. He'd withheld from the wars his only heir, an unruly and wayward boy, an undisciplined dreamer, a woe to his late mother. Now he was clearly deranged, flame infected, and unstable. The king withdrew his sword from its scabbard. He'd teach the boy a lesson if that's what it took. The whelp would learn to respect him and do his duty.

Bent-kneed and circling, the king whooshed his sword through the air, beheading a cluster of midnight daisies. He was fast for forty, retaining most of the vigor of his youth. In contrast, though young and brawny, Gordan was heavy on his feet and not overly nimble.

"You think you'll best me, boy? Don't be too sure. I tutored your fencing. I know *all* your weaknesses."

"But you don't know your own!" Gordan lunged forward. Steel clattered against steel, releasing sparks. Blow followed blow, each blocking the other. The king swiveled into a new position for another strike, but Gordan parried and knocked the blade from his grasp. The king gasped in amazement. Gordan swung behind him, booting the back of his knee, caving in his leg, then pushing him forward, plunging him to the earth.

The king landed hard on his face, mouth in the dirt. He tasted warm blood, felt the pang of a knocked-out tooth. Writhing, he spat it out of his mouth. He reached for his boot with the secret dagger, always laced with poison, just in case.

"No, stop!" The voice was sweet as a midnight rose. "You will not harm him."

The king turned. Flower Strong stood in the cottage doorway, hallowed in candlelight. She stepped out, bent over, and opened her hand as if rolling a ball his way. Flames shot out of her fingertips.

The burning began in the king's toes. It spread to his ankles, calves, then crept up the length of his thighs to his groin and midriff until he was completely engulfed.

Flower Strong rose back up, hands balled. Tears streamed down her cheeks.

Blue sparks exploded. Firecrackers and flames filled the breeze, cascading down, strewing petals and leaves.

"Enough! Enough!" The king slithered about, grasping at bramble, clawing up weeds, desperate to escape the flames. "I'm not a monster! I wouldn't hurt him! He's my son!" But the fire continued its course, unrelenting. It wouldn't kill him. It wouldn't even harm him. But it would teach him respect. The fire would have its way.

"You plotted to murder me," Flower Strong said. "I trusted you, revered you."

"I repent!" King Alvon said.

"Love is a mystery," Flower Strong said. "Can't you understand? It is wretched and knows no reason. But it rights every wrong. It comes from above. It is the way."

"I repent!"

Flower Strong turned to Gordan with a melancholy sigh. "You must do what's best for your people and marry Felicity. Lives are at stake."

"But you're the one I want, Flower Strong."

"*I* will propose to Felicity," King Alvon said. "*I* will marry her. Oh, I'm in love! I love her! I love her! I love her!"

The flames died. The moon floated out from behind its cloud cover, and a hoot owl sounded from the trees.

"Father," Gordan said, coming to his aid. "Are you injured?"

"Get your hands off me! I've a wedding to plan!"

Orc

None would speak to me but the outcast from the village, worn and weary, scented of weed-lore and brimstone, always busy by the cauldron at her hearth. They said of me *no heart* . . .

But she simply warned me, hoary brows twitching, itching at her whiskered beauty mark, "Do not go down that long, long road from which there is no return."

And yet, such restlessness to roam possessed me! The weird woman tried to wizen me: "Hold your head up!" But heaviness weighted me like a dark flower drooping into the gloom.

"Don't wreck yourself," said the hag. "Do you want to be like me?" I trod down into the forbidden valley, where tulips bloom black as midnight, their fragrance just as terrible. "Choose the day!" she said.

I dove into shadows, basked in the hollows, thrived by moonlight, shunning the garish glimmer of sunshine on still waters. Like a sea beast, big-eyed and tentacled, I longed for depths. I watched clouds drift over the moon upon a patch of magic mushrooms. I soaked up enchantment's chill mist, unchecked as any beast, fanged as the damned.

Love—impossible, despised. I cursed and bristled like wild thistle . . .

I have found that the road, indeed, is long. None can return. Let's not say, *damned*, but *lost* without a home.

Still, some days I see it—sunlight blazing over the mountains in the Land of the Living.

The Teacher

In the year of the long-haired star, an old man came to our village. The cosmos glittered in his flaming eyes. He spoke of hope and healing, blessings and boons. He owled us unmercifully with proverbs and pleas. We laughed at him inwardly, but, amused and grinning, asked that he tell us more, bid him stay awhile.

Parables rolled off the old man's tongue and teachings foolishly wise. He spoke of life everlasting in a voice like thunder and urged us not to worship the dragon. Then our smiles faded, for such devotion was our custom. "What value would there be in such irreverence?" one man piped up, and among the throng, heads nodded, grunts agreed. "How can I even be a man and not worship the dragon?" another asked, and none disagreed. The old man walked away, westward, his head neither high nor bowed.

Weeks later, I ascended the mountain, though my betters had warned me never to approach the dragon's lair. Just past the tree line, the dark mouth loomed. I lit my torch and entered. I strode all the way to the back, explored every crack and cranny, only to confirm my worst suspicions. My religion was baseless. No foul beast occupied the dank tomb, not so much as a garden snake, only stalactites and a lonely dripping.

Disillusioned, determined to discern ultimate Truth, I packed my bindle. I set my course, heading westward like the old man. I walked into the night. I pilgrimaged down hallowed roads. I traveled through time, passed into starlight, silvered into that old man.

I arrived back at the village of my birth, finding myself, a young lad with laughing eyes, sleet-stung cheeks, and a skeptical grin, barely able to listen.

The Two Princes

A Fairy Tale Novelette

Chapter 1

The Princess
and the Eunuch

"Why can't I go?" Princess Perqueena lay on her stomach on the bed. She thrashed about, furs and pink silk wrinkling up beneath her.

Three candles fizzled along the shelf, dispensing light and an apple-cinnamon aroma throughout the castle bedchamber. Outside the window on an oak branch a screech owl hooted.

"Your parents have said you cannot attend the royal ball," Gareb, the eunuch, announced in alto. Perqueena's personal bodyguard, he sat on a stool, blocking the doorway, determined not to budge, preventing her escape. In previous squabbles concerning her curfew, Perqueena had warred to bodily remove him from that post, yet husky Gareb always proved as immobile as a boulder, even when Perqueena broke priceless vases over his now-scarred baldness. *Perhaps she's finally abandoned violent methods to her ends*, Gareb hoped, jaw clenched.

Perqueena stopped kicking. "I'm thirteen, old enough to go to the ball!" She punched the mattress. Then, calming, she peered up at the reflection in the mirror of her ivory vanity, strewn with bejeweled combs, oriental colognes, silk flowers . . . and a jar of grub beetles with holes in the lid. "Let me go anyway. I'll sneak downstairs and enter the ballroom through the back door when nobody is looking." A nasal laugh erupted through the prominent nose inherited from her father. Her nose. The one feature she felt sensitive about, a sentiment fancy gowns and expensive jewelry typically remedied. She bit a fingernail then farted loudly, laughing at the breach in propriety she allowed herself in private when dukes and duchesses weren't there to admire her. "Yes, just let me go anyway!" She kicked her feet up behind her, dreaming of getting her way.

"I can't let you do that, Your Highness."

"Phooey! Why not?" Perqueena rolled onto her side, her pale blue evening gown twisting around her narrow body, her silver slippers sliding off her feet. Hand beneath her head, diamond necklace falling between budding cleavage, she glared at him, eyes flashes of angry fire.

Ah, the pinch! The uncomfortable feeling of knowing he couldn't please both Perqueena and her parents. To chaperone a disgruntled princess, to be kicked and punched and pelted with flying objects was difficult enough, yet to defy her parent's express instructions could warrant the death penalty. Somehow, the former seemed the lesser of two evils.

"Your Queen Mother thinks you should wait a year or two before flirting with all those dukes and barons then dashing their hopes to pieces." Gareb adjusted his weight on the stool.

"Two years?" Perqueena rolled off the bed and sat down at her vanity. "Two Years? That's forever! I'll be a hag before she'll let me do *anything*! It'll *never* be my turn!" She picked up a jar of lip gloss, unscrewed the cap, dabbed her finger into the oily tint, then besmeared anew her lower lip.

"You're barely out of the cradle." Gareb wiped his moist palms along his woolen britches.

"Why can't I celebrate our squashing of the peasant's rebellion with the rest of the aristocracy?" Perqueena picked up her blush brush to accent again the rosy apples of her cheeks.

"I believe your King Father prefers to term this night a 'peace celebration.'"

Perqueena threw down the blush brush with a huff. "I want to watch Wurwick the Wizard cast spooky spells. I want to see Jackimo the Jester juggle golden balls. I want to laugh at the kitchen wenches bustling about the banquet table."

I want! I want! I want! Gareb gnashed his teeth. Sometimes he wished Perqueena would die in her sleep. Her desires were a bottomless pit that could never be filled. The more lavished upon her, the more she demanded. In the three years he'd served her, he'd longed for her character to blossom into something beautiful, but it hadn't seemed to, and he feared it never would.

He forced his lips into a practiced smile. "I understand how you feel, but you're just too young to be a debutant."

"I want to see what color Prince Caspian of Bohemia is wearing, and who he dances with!" Perqueena strode to the window and peered down the viny brick to the dimly lit darkness below.

"If you'll only be patient, Your Majesty, in a few years that person shall be *you*! You'll be the most stunning creature on the dance floor!"

"I want to feel champagne bubbles fizz beneath my nose. I can smell the roast boar, yet I'm locked up here starving." She turned away from the window.

"You had plenty for supper." Gareb moved his stool closer to the door. "In a few years, Your Majesty, you may go."

"I want to go *now*!" Perqueena stomped her foot, her eyes disappearing into horizontal slits.

Gareb knew that tone of voice. He ran his hand across his dome, wiping away beads of apprehension.

"Move that fat butt off the stool and let me out!" Perqueena grabbed a lacy throw pillow from the bed and hurled it at him with all her might.

Whew! Only a pillow! Gareb ducked. He remembered the last priceless vase shattering across his head. "More than anything in the world, I wish I could let you. Believe me; I share your pain."

"Puppa gives me leave to pick from among the eunuch vassals. I could always find a funner fellow to gloat over my imprisonment, and that's all this is too." Scowling, she sat back down at her vanity. "I could have you demoted, and you know what happens to castoff eunuchs." She peered back at him.

"Slooooop!" Gareb sliced his finger across his neck. "They fall straight through The Booby Trap down into the darkest recesses of Hell!" He laughed nervously, hoping Perqueena wouldn't be *that* cruel were her displeasure to worsen. He knew as well as she the kingdom treated unkindly servants who lost their posts.

"No, even worse. The are banished to the mines to spend the rest of their days in the dimly lit dark where they forget forever the pleasure of sunlight and fresh air!" With one hand Perqueena scrunched her tawny waste of curls, fixed upon her image in the glass.

Gareb shivered. "Surely, Your Highness, you must realize I indulge your fancies as much as I'm allowed. You'd fair no better were any other person assigned to protect you. Your parents have spoken, and you should have mercy on poor old Gareb. I grovel at your feet! I worship you like a god . . ."

"God*dess*!" She opened then slammed shut the drawer of her vanity, searching in vain for miscellaneous toiletry.

"I care for nothing but your happiness."

Perqueena rolled her eyes. "Then let me go to the ball, and don't tell my parents." She smiled sweetly at him through the mirror.

A drop of sweat rolled down Gareb's cheek beside the metallic earring. "Do you realize what you're asking me to do? To be an accomplice to your rebellion, to disobey your parents' orders, I'd risk *execution*. It would be an act of sedition! I'd prefer to live, if you'll be so gracious as to forgive me for saying." He pressed his fingers together and bowed his crisscrossed head.

"Humph! What's one life compared to a night at the ball?"

"Perqueena?" Gareb said.

She ducked her head. Then she jumped back on the mattress, rolled onto her stomach, and broke wind again. "Then what am I to do this evening? I'm so bored it's killing me! I want some entertainment!" She bounded off the bed again and hastened to the window. Peering down, her face bloomed into a sly grin! "Maybe I'll tie a sheet to my bedpost and climb out the window." She touched a pink silk canopy curtain, scheming.

Gareb leaned forward on his stool. "I'd think not! You'd fall into the rose bushes and cut yourself on the thorns! You'd be scarred beyond recognition! Prince Caspian would faint at the very sight of you!"

Perqueena's gleeful expression withered. She slumped back onto the bed, wilted.

The bedchamber grew silent. Downstairs, violins blended with flutes and mandolins. Crystal goblets, bubbling with sparkling wine, clinked. Men and women laughed, gliding across the dance floor, satin dresses rustling. Outside the window, on the streets, horses neighed. The scents of honeysuckle and roses whooshed through the bedchamber window with the warm summer breeze, stirring the gossamer curtains.

"Perhaps you might be in the mood for a delightful story?" Gareb said. "Have you heard the tale of Violet and Daisy?

"Who?" Perqueena turned, offering her snobbiest stare.

"Two village girls in a story I'd like to tell you, a tale my old nanny told me as a youth, one of my favorites, and a true story at that, or so she swore." It was just the thing to pacify Perqueena. For any other folly she possessed, she did enjoy enchanting tales.

"A story?" Perqueena peered at him with raised brow, sampling the bait like a worm at a fishhook.

"Yes, I know just the story to tell you!" He licked his chapped lips. "Why would any princess want to attend a boring, old ball with all those sour-faced boobies and spoiled old poops when she could hear a delightful tale, told by her very favorite eunuch?"

Perqueena shrugged. "I don't know. Maybe. Is it a good story?"

"The best story imaginable!"

"Does it have a princess in it?"

"Not at first, though both girls marry royalty later."

"Why should I care about two spoiled princesses who probably get to go to the ball every single night when I *never* will?"

"The story is not all balls and splendors, Your Highness."

"How so?" Curiosity glimmered in her eyes.

"One of the girls faces a terrible problem. I bet you'd be curious to find out what."

"So, this really will be a good story?"

"If it's not the very best story you've ever heard, Your Majesty, full of conflict, conquest, and controversy, then *slooooop*!" His finger slid across his neck.

Perqueena laughed, cheeks dimpling. She curled her legs up against her torso, hugging her knees.

"Splendid!" Gareb clapped his hands together then rubbed them to warmth. "It seems Her Highness wants to hear the story!"

"I'll *try* to listen. But it had better be the best story in the world, *or else!*"

"It will be, Your Highness. Promise." Gareb felt relieved his plan was succeeding, though now he faced the challenge of remembering details of a story he hadn't contemplated for years. He'd just have to invent what he'd forgotten. He did some quick thinking then began: "Once upon a time, there lived an honest woodcutter and his two lovely daughters, Violet and Daisy—"

"Wait," Perqueena cut in. "Are Violet and Daisy whores because I don't want to hear a story about whores because whores are tiresome, or that's what Puppa says."

Gareb shook his head. "Your Highness, I assure you, Violet and Daisy are certainly not whores, too complicated for words, but acceptable for your ears."

Perqueena studied her crimson fingernails. "Well, if you're sure."

"Shall I proceed with the story?"

Perqueena shrugged, but then peered up with eyes shining attentively, betraying a genuine interest. She squirmed into her nook of minks. "Go on then."

Gareb cleared his throat then began . . .

Chapter 2

The Woodcutter's Daughters

Once upon a time, there lived an honest woodcutter and his two lovely daughters, Violet and Daisy. Their cottage stood just inside the forest on the outskirts of the kingdom. The king was a just ruler, though old and tired, and had recently pledged his throne to his fraternal twin sons and divided the boundaries between them. In return, his sons had sworn an oath to always rule the people justly.

Each day in the summer, after finishing their chores, Violet and Daisy would leave their cottage and walk through the fields to gather wildflowers or berries for their father. He loved such gifts from his daughters almost as much as he loved them. Daisy had always been a well-behaved girl, though Violet was known to be contrary. Yet the old wood-cutter loved them both.

One sunny summer day Violet and Daisy were strolling through the fields as usual when a strange white beast crept out from the forbidden forest on the other side of the field.

A horn shot straight up from its downy forehead and coiled around like a twist of bread, coming to a blunted tip. The air shimmered all about him as if he were magical.

Daisy gasped. "What an unusual beast!"

"I've never seen an animal sparkle," Violet said.

"Maybe he'll let us stroke his soft white head," Daisy said.

"Yes, let's make friends with him!" Violet agreed.

They ran up to the gentle beast that seemed to nod his head in accord. He let them stroke his nose, as docile as a kitten. Then off he darted, disappearing into the forbidden forest as quickly as he'd emerged, leaving just a few branches rustling.

"Where's he gone?" Daisy asked.

"Maybe he wants us to follow him," Violet said. "Perhaps he'll lead us somewhere magical! With princes and castles and glamor and glitz!"

"Hold on, "Daisy said. "Those woods are forbidden. Father has always warned us to not venture into those shadowy depths."

"Don't be such a sorry poop," Violet chided, contrary as ever. "I'll take all the blame should Father scold us. Now come on!" She yanked on Daisy's sleeve.

Reluctantly, despite her better judgement, Daisy tagged along after Violet. She couldn't let her sister wander off alone, contrary as she was.

Soon, finding a trail to follow, the two sisters were racing through the forbidden forest. Violet took the lead, eager for the enchantment promised by the strange beast. Soon she forgot all about her father's warnings not to venture where she ought not.

Oh yes, those woods were wild, full of howls and yellow eyes that glowed at night! The gnomes who lived there distrusted big folk. Their magic was peculiar and unpredictable. And the goblins had always proven unspeakable to every traveler they snared. But Violet simply had to find that magical beast, so on she ran, Daisy right behind her. Deeper and deeper into the wilderness they tarried, each step they took a frightful risk.

Gradually, the underbrush began to choke off the trail till the path grew obscure and nebulous. Then, suddenly . . .

Squish!

Violet froze. The sound was moist, repulsive. She peered down at her leather shoe. The mess was all over it. A foul scent wafted up into her nostrils. Violet lifted her foot, examining the mess, then peered back at Daisy.

When Daisy saw the mess, horror flooded her face. She gasped, hand to her mouth. "Violet, you've stepped in goblin dung! That's six years bad luck!"

"Goblin dung?" Violet withered, dismayed. A sob left her throat. "Oh Daisy, we shouldn't have come here! Why didn't you stop me? Now I'm cursed!"

"Throw your shoes away," Daisy said. "Maybe, somehow, you can avoid the curse."

"How does one break free from a curse?" Violet asked, stepping out of her blighted footwear and tossing them into the brambles. "I fear for certain doom!"

Chapter 3

The Gnome

How loathsome the woods seemed to Violet, now that she was six years cursed. "Oh, this is terrible, terrible," she wailed, flailing her arms.

"Perhaps I can help," a deep voice said.

Daisy and Violet peered all about, but they saw nobody. "Who's there?" Violet said, wishing she had a pocketknife.

"Show yourself!" Daisy said.

"Here I am. Look down and over," the voice spoke again.

The girls turned. A gnome, not more than eight inches high, stood on a fallen log. He wore soft leather and a pale linen cap, his nut-brown face broad, about his mouth a profusion of silvery whiskers. He pointed at Violet's discarded shoes and shook his head. "You should have watched your step, young lady." He wagged his finger. "Your careless trespass has earned you six years bad luck!"

Violet moaned with dismay. "I know! I know! Oh, how can I endure it?"

"Perhaps my magic can help." The gnome presented a clever grin.

Violet clasped her hands together. "Oh, please! Name your price!" she stammered hastily, forgetting her father's teaching that bestowing gratitude is often enough.

Violet's shoulders sagged. "We don't have any money, little fellow. We are simple woodcutter's daughters."

"Call me Hobblecrank," said the gnome. "We forest folk don't use coinage. We barter. What do you have, small and light, that I can carry?"

Violet pondered, brow furrowed. Then she snapped her fingers. "I've got it!" She reached into her skirt pocket and retrieved a wad of red yarn left over from a knitting project. "How about this beautiful red yarn?" She held it forward.

Hobblecrank gasped with appreciation. Then he snatched up the wad, pressing the fibers between his thick fingers. "This I can use on my spindle! This can cancel two years of curse!" He opened his leather purse, stowed away the wad, and retrieved a little twig. "This is my magic wand," he said then drew it through the air, strewing glittery stardust all about. It flittered over Violet and spilled onto the earth around her.

"That tingles," Violet said, holding out her hands like a child in snowflakes. "I can feel it working!"

"What else do you have?" Hobblecrank asked.

Violet turned her pockets inside out. "Oh dear, I've nothing left to give you!"

"How about my lace bracelet?" Daisy asked, unfastening its mother-of-pearl clasp and slipping it from her wrist in consideration of her sister's predicament.

"How very generous of you to help your sister," Hobblecrank said. "I'll take it!"

"Oh, Daisy! Thank you!" Violet said as Daisy bent down to give Hobblecrank her one piece of finery.

Hobblecrank opened his backpack and stowed away the lace. Then he waved his magic wand through the air again. Another burst of glitter spurted from the tip, cascading over Violet, a few sparkles even landing on Daisy.

"Now a full four years of the curse are melted away," Hobblecrank said, still holding aloft his wand. "What else will you give me? Only two years of curse remain. What more will you gift me?"

"More? You want more?" Violet asked, growing frustrated. "Haven't we given you enough already?"

"How about that big yellow button on the pocket of your shirt?" Hobblecrank asked, eyes dark and glassy.

"This old thing?" Violet looked down at the button just as a tiny sparkle of magic seeped into it. Suddenly, the scuffed fastener seemed too wondrous to behold. Violet held her hand over the button as if it were her heart. "Surely, you wouldn't ask such a dear price, little sir! That wouldn't be fair!"

"Selfish girl," Hobblecrank said. "I need that button for a wheel. Doubt not I'll put it to good use. Now give it to me, and in exchange, my magic will make you completely curse free."

"Oh please, not my beautiful yellow button!" Violet peered all about the woods, searching for solutions. "How about a lace from my one good shoe?" She pointed toward the discarded pair under the brambles.

"Those shoes are both bad luck now, and my magic is costly," Hobblecrank said. "Draining my reserves comes at a fair price. Now give me that button, or we are through bartering."

Violet stomped her foot. "You miserable little miser! I'd sooner cut off my right hand and give that to you!"

"Give him the button!" Daisy said, ready to tear one from her own pocket.

"Can't I have anything nice?" Violet flailed her arms.

Hobblecrank's nut brown face tinted orange as a harvest moon. He stamped his little slipper on the log. "Foolish girl! You'll be sorry!" Then, in a puff of green smoke, he vanished from the woods.

"Wait! Don't go," Violet said, stumbling toward the log, but it was too late.

"He's gone," Daisy said, shoulders slumping. "Along with most of the curse, but not all." She sighed wearily. "You should have given him that button."

"You're right. I don't know what came over me." Violet clutched her head. "His magic made me dizzy, clouded my thinking. And now it's too late."

"Forget about it," Daisy said. "We need to get home. We've wasted the whole day on idle fancies. Think how mad Father will be if we haven't returned before sunset!"

"And yet, I'm just exhausted," Violet said. "Let's rest a moment first, on that patch of moss beneath the oak." She pointed into the dusky depths, laden with mysterious stirrings. "We'll be safe. Goblins only come out between midnight and the witching hour."

"I hate to delay our return, but I'm weary too." Daisy nodded. "Let's hope there are no spiders." And so, with Violet walking more carefully on her bare feet, they strode further off the path to the moss. There, there lay down and soon fell fast asleep.

Chapter 4

The Two Princes

Near to where Daisy and Violet were sleeping, the king's fraternal twin sons, Justin and Damon, were roaming field and forest to hunt or loiter. Damon's fiery eyes were fierce and piercing, and he kept a sword at his belt in case some foe might happen to attack him. Justin's eyes were bright and shining, and he carried a bow across his back in hopes his sportsmanship might catch him a hart.

"What a beautiful day," Justin said, beaming. "And what a lovely scent coming from the woods, just like a flower garden!"

"I smell nothing but my own sweaty body." Damon scowled, wiping his brow with a dirty glove.

But Justin only inhaled more deeply then stepped forward through the trees. He moved past a clump of bushes and parted the hanging mosses. There lay Violet and Daisy, fast asleep! Though their hair was tousled and their peasant dresses simple, the girls were lovely to behold. Violet's gypsy-black braid nestled against her frame, and Daisy's locks of gold spilled freely down her back. They huddled together like two turtledoves, Violet barefoot, enchantment from the woods glittering all about them.

Justin gazed at Violet then his eyes moved to Daisy. When he saw her sweet face, peace flooded his soul, and he fell in love with her instantly.

Damon moved up behind him. His fierce eyes roved over the moss. His gaze fixed on Violet, and his muscles tightened.

"Hush," Justin whispered, finger to his lips.

Just then, Violet opened her eyes, as if startled by a dream. She gasped at the intruders, waking Daisy with a shake. They bounded to their feet, wiping twigs and pine needles from their aprons.

"You must be lords," Daisy said, noting their shiny boots and fancy velvet blouses.

"We've caught you, trespassing in the king's forest," Damon growled.

"Yet have no fear," Justin added, taking Daisy's hand and helping her step off the moss. "You've done no wrong, and no wrong will come to you."

Daisy looked into Justin's face and saw the kindness in his eyes. "You're such a gentleman. You must be a prince!"

Seeing that she recognized his virtue, Justin was so smitten he lifted her hand and kissed it. "In truth, I *am* a prince. And you, most definitely, are a lady. Come dine at my table tonight!"

"How can I refuse such a wondrous offer?" Daisy gasped, delighted, peering but briefly at Violet.

Justin escorted her to the tree where he and Damon had tied their horses. He whisked her onto his white steed, Champion, then climbed up behind her.

"Goodbye Violet! See you soon," Daisy said with a carefree smile as she and Justin rode away, leaving Violet and Damon alone.

"Are you a gentleman too?" Violet asked.

Damon huffed with irritation. "I'm prince! Prince of this whole realm!" He threw out his arm. "You should have recognized that immediately and known not to trespass on my hunting grounds. All this belongs to me—every acorn, every blade of grass, every trespasser and trespass—it's mine, all mine, so now you'll have to come with me!" He grabbed her wrist rather roughly and pulled her toward his black stallion, Thunder.

"I'm very sorry," Violet said, trying in vain to wrench herself free. "I meant no harm. I will made amends."

"Indeed, you will, troublesome wench," Damon glowered back at her.

Chapter 5

The Wedding Feast

Damon and Violet rode through the open fields on horseback then arrived at an ivy-covered castle. The sun was just setting behind the horizon and the crickets just beginning to sing their mournful song. At the drawbridge door, Damon lifted Violet from his horse and left the beast with a stable hand.

"My father will wonder where I am," Violet said.

"I'll send him word," Damon replied. "I must be frank, dear girl. I feel strangely drawn to you, although you are a commoner. You've cast a spell on me. Of that, I'm sure. Doubt not there will be consequences!"

"I beg your pardon, sir, but I am not a witch!" Violet said, as candid and polite as she could muster.

Damon huffed. "Come inside." He led her into the darkened structure, lit with candles. Then the door slammed shut like a beartrap.

"Truth be told, I'm growing fond of you, despite my better judgement," Damon curtly told her. "Little witch! Now,

I'll be your lord and master. Now, you'll be mistress of this castle!"

"I am not what you say I am," Violet said as the servants sniggered.

"Tonight, I'm hosting a banquet for all the lords and ladies of the land. Every person of importance I have invited," Damon said, his face a boastful sneer. "Tonight, I'll display you as my new prized possession. Tonight, will be our wedding feast! Tonight, you will become my Dragon Lady!" Eyes wild, he bellowed and clapped at the servants, hastening them to resume preparations.

Soon, before Violet even knew what to say, servant girls were arraying her in a black silk gown. Damon placed upon her wrists silver bracelets, coiled into serpents. Monstrous horns sprang from her headdress, supporting a dark, flowing veil. But the costume only made Violet feel ugly. The bracelets were heavy, like a warrior's gauntlets. The dress pinched, so she could hardly breathe. And the headdress made her temples ache. She felt like she was headed to a funeral. Black seemed to be Damon's favorite color.

"Soon my guests will arrive," Damon said. "Come with me!" He led her by the hand across the stone floor to the mead hall, where torches glowed and servants scurried about the table, filling to overflow with delicacies.

Damon seated Violet beside him near the head of the table just as the servants admitted the first couples through the front door. In strode lords and ladies in lavish garments of every imaginable color. The feasting began. Wine flowed. Jugglers tossed up red rubber balls, while the jesters laughed, stuck out their tongues like gargoyles, and turned over and over in summersaults down the expansive hall. Warlocks chanted incantations, casting spooky spells with a smoky poof. Bards and pipers kept the melody, and Damon chuckled like a demon!

The guests seemed dazzled. Ladies swooned against their escorts in aristocratic ecstasy. But Violet felt dizzy from the smoke and antics, fingers at her temple, sick and bewildered.

Damon rose from his seat with a wine-filled goblet. "Lords and ladies." He tapped his plate with a fork, holding the cup forward. "I propose a toast to the kingdom. May none other be mighty as mine. May all who speak one evil word of her be crushed and plundered and left as food for the vultures!"

"To the kingdom," a duke chimed in.

"To the vultures!" a jocund baron bantered, igniting the room with laughter.

As the mirth faded, the guests raised their goblets and drank. But the wine tasted bitter to poor, befuddled Violet. Reveling in his ascension to the moment, Damon forgot to even introduce her. But she pushed up a smile, sipping from a wine goblet servants refilled faster than she could even drink. Soon, in fact, she was miserably drunk and reeling. Yet the revelry had only begun.

Chapter 6

The Curse

Violet awoke the next day in a bedchamber, high above an alligator-filled mote. Oh, how her head ached. The air was stuffy, and no scent of wildflowers passed through the window to refresh her as it had each morning outside her woodland home.

Outside the door, heavy boots thudded on the stairs. Rusted metal tried the keyhole. Then the door sprang open like the jaws of a dragon. There stood Damon, dark eyes glimmering like a dragon-master.

"I've brought you breakfast." He grinned, holding up a tray. "Breakfast in bed. You'll have nothing but chocolates to eat! Now that you're my special lady, I plan to spoil you rotten!" He placed the tray on her lap.

"Have you sent word to my father? Does Daisy know I'm here? May I go into the forest and pick berries and wildflowers?"

"Flowers don't grow here. And the only berries are poisonous. Forget such thoughts. You must stay put!" Then, before she could ask further questions, Damon departed the room, leaving Violet alone with her sweetmeats.

In the days that followed, Damon fed Violet nothing but cakes and candies to keep her lulled and quiet. He told her gothic legends. He performed true acrobatics, frolicking in foolscap and cane. He flaunted his pet snake, Lucifer. "I'm a fanatic," he ranted. "I'm a hellhound," he panted. "I'm a were-wolf," he howled, slipping on another guise. "Perhaps I'm just too pretty," he taunted, batting an amorous eye. "Sometimes I'm a little bit shy. I'm a perfect specimen," he boasted. "I'm an arrogant wild boar," he bristled, burning and flickering like fire. "No, you don't have to respect me," he badgered, stripping and whipping his bashful bride. "I don't mean to mash you," he bullied, caressing a shimmering thigh. "You must stop squirming!" He crushed and bruised, cruising with a twist and a gyre. "I'd prefer to have you happy," he gloated, "Maybe I'm a super nice guy!" The cultic guru pacified and christened, glistening like a star in the sky. "When will you stop nagging," he jived and jittered, plucking on a golden lyre. He tried every artful tactic imaginable to get poor Violet to thrive. He sought to stupefy her, dancing and prancing about the canopy like Pan, but Violet never even smiled. Then one day her listless stupor enraged him. "I warn you, Violet, you *must* love me, or you will come to die!"

Violet doubted that she could but sought to appease him. "Of course, daring dearest," she said, feeling gloomy and accursed.

Soon, all was amiss in the land. Wars broke out on the outskirts of the kingdom. The people became distempered and quarrelsome, but Damon didn't understand why. Cows weren't producing milk. Chickens weren't laying eggs, and Damon couldn't fathom it. Nor could he understand why storm clouds always hovered over his castle, yet no rain came to wash the land.

One afternoon, he went upstairs to visit Violet, and his mouth fell open with dismay. Her hair had lost its luster, her rosy cheeks had paled, and her glistening eyes had dimmed, surrounded by dark circles.

"Damon, I'm sick," she said. "I fear it's just as you say. I am going to die."

"You'll recover," he said and hastened away to summon a doctor.

But neither surgeons nor leaches could help poor Violet to recover. She languished to the point that she couldn't even get out of bed in the morning. She stayed under the sheets, sweating and whimpering. Damon clenched his jaw, hand fisting. "I must do something drastic, or I'll lose my prized possession!" Then a dark plan flickered into his mind.

Chapter 7

The Witch

Just as the sun was sinking in the west, and the last streaks of flaming gold were fading from the horizon, Damon left the castle on horseback, his black cape flapping behind him like a vampire.

He arrived at a cottage beneath a knoll just outside the forest's edge. There lived a witch few people dared accost. She would have the answer to his problem with Violet, or so he supposed.

Damon tied his horse to the gnarled branch of a twisted oak then knocked on the witch's door. The weird woman, Agatha, emerged from the gloom. Old crone though she was, she enhanced her appearance with a spell of beauty, yet unconvincingly like an obvious wig. Beneath her guise withered a weathered face, all warty, and hair straw-like as a scarecrow. A distinct foulness lurked within her core. Yet the spell softened her aspect, lending charm, and Damon let the ruse appease him.

Agatha's eyes popped at the sight of him. "Come in! Come in! What can I do for you? And how will you pay?"

she said, lusty and eager, lunging forward to clutch Damon with her thick-knuckled fingers, stained with spellcasting.

"Stand back!" He pushed aside her claw. "This is strictly business. You know I'm Prince, and you must do my bidding. Now, listen. Mistress Mine is sick. She's waxing rancid as a toad, and I *must* find a cure for her condition."

"Is that all?" Agatha cackled with amusement. "She's just one of these girls who has a problem with her father. The cure for such measles is really quite simple. All you need to do is frighten off her rebellion. Now come and taste my brew; then you'll see what you must do!"

Damon glanced at the bubbling cauldron, the caged black crow, the columns of dead bats, dangling from the rotted roof, and his knees wobbled. The atmosphere seemed to sizzle like a thunderbolt. Even for him, the hovel was terrible.

"Come and taste my brew, and you will have a vision," Agatha said as Damon approached the cauldron. "Little old me? Oh no," she scolded. "Not in this rag; you know better than that!" she hustled. "Just let me add the last wiles to these wicked, old bubbles."

"Make it snappy," Damon said, warry of her greed and perversity.

"All things in due season," Agatha said, touching her fingertips to her lips, as if bashful of a blench, then tilted her head back with cackling.

In went the frog legs, spider webs, and toad gruel. In went the wiggly worms, rat tail, and all the manna of dead things Damon couldn't recognize and didn't want to.

"Try it. It's tasty!" Agatha smacked her lips, raising a wooden spoon to his paling mouth.

Damon knew he must dare a sip, and so he did. "Mmmm." His brows rose at the complex flavor, more enjoyable than he'd expected. But then his heart raced and his mind blackened. "Enough!" he said as she raised another spoonful.

"Now you quit that. You're being terrible." Agatha grinned and bloated.

Damon stood resolute. "No more! I know what to do. I have seen a vision. I've no more use for you." He sped from the cottage as Agatha followed.

"Why leave so soon? The night could get cozy! Sit down by my hearth and get yourself toasty. What did I say? Did I make you uncomfortable? I'm not too fancy, so don't be so testy. Come back here right now, and let Nanna touch you!" The old sorceress crooned and crooned, but Damon mounted his steed and rode off with the shadows, disappearing into the forest depths.

Chapter 8

The Peasant

Damon neared the mote, his revelation from the witch's brew burning within him. He needed a peasant to do his worst. His gaze shifted to a door along the side of the castle: the prison. He left his mount with a stable hand and approached the door. He chose one key from a ring at his belt and fed it to the lock then stepped down into the dungeon.

Damon found the guard sleeping on a stool with a wine bottle tucked beneath his arm and chicken bones scattered across the floor. "Wake up, you worthless drunkard!" Damon booted him.

The guard's lids rolled open like the eyes of a big bullfrog. "Your Majesty?" His posture stiffened with alarm.

"Release this prisoner!" Damon pointed to the nearest cubicle where a chained peasant in filthy rags sat on befouled straw, head hunched over. "Release him at once!"

The soul behind bars peered up. "Me? Oh, thank you, Lord Damon! My family will be so glad to see me. I only stole the fish pie because we were starving."

"Quiet," Damon said. "You deserve death, but I've chosen mercy. Now, you must do my bidding."

"Oh, I'll do anything!"

"First, you'll come with me."

"Thank you, Your Grace! Thank you!"

The guard unlocked the prison cell door. Damon led the peasant, limping along behind him, up the stairs and into the castle, quiet from the late hours. Then, up the next flight of stairs they climbed toward the bedchamber.

"Where are you taking me?" the peasant asked.

"You'll see," Damon said. "First, you must bathe. Then I'll release you."

"A bath?" the peasant asked, puzzling.

Damon opened the door to the bedchamber where Violet lay in a deathly doze. The full moon shone through the window, but Damon lit a candle, releasing an eerie glow.

"Dump your rags out the window and get in that tub." Damon pointed to the copper basin in the corner.

The peasant, still puzzling, discarded his rags then eased his tortured bones into the tub. "Where's the water?" he asked.

"Patience," Damon said. He slipped behind him. He removed the dagger from his belt. He raised the blade. Then he plunged it down into the scrawny back with all his might. The scream pierced the darkness then faded into oblivion.

Blood gushed from the body into the basin, under a full moon and stars, while the crickets sang their mournful song. When the tub was full, Damon broke the bars from the crumbly rock window then tossed the corpse into the moat for the alligators.

Violet groaned, swooning with delirium.

"What's wrong, my sweet?" Damon asked with unusual gentility, hastening to the bedside, hands bloody.

"What are you doing? That smell. Like a slaughtered animal. It turns my stomach."

"Don't be such a spoiled child." Damon tapped her nose with his finger, leaving a crimson stain. "Now come. I must bathe you," he said, for a blood bath was the prescription of the witch's brew, what he'd seen in his vision.

Just as his vision had inspired him, Damon baptized his prized possession in a pool of fresh blood, hoping to slough off her illness, despite her weak protests to the contrary. When he finished, he rinsed Violet with water and helped her back to bed. He dumped the tub's contents out the window with a pitcher. He left the rest of the mess to a castle-keeper, explaining the stains as the work of a blood-letter. Afterwards, weary though sleepless, he went downstairs for a sausage sandwich.

But despite the blood bath therapy, Violet's condition worsened. Screams echoed from her blood-stained window. Deep into the night, travelers heard her terrible cries. Sores broke out across her sorrowful body, and pain wrecked her very soul with agony.

Chapter 9

The Friar

Early one balmy summer morn, a sensitive diplomatic mission, which he refused to discuss with Violet, took Prince Damon away from the castle, leaving her alone with the servants. She lay in bed, her head swirling with fever, her double vision dizzying her. Every muscle in her body ached, and her skin looked like a cadaver's.

A whistling noise outside her window broke through her stupor. She sat up in bed, her head high enough to peer out the blood-stained window.

A friar, seeming merry from his smile and the upbeat melody, was trapsing down the grassy climb on the trail leading to the castle. His dark hair freshly shaven to bald, he wore a loose-sleeved brown tunic falling to his ankles and tied at his cumbersome waist with twine. Violet soon inferred he was a eunuch, for he was tall, wide-hipped, and breasted like a woman. He resembled other eunuchs she'd seen on occasion in the village near the cottage of her birth.

At the sight of the friar, Violet gasped with surprise. Why would any holy person venture anywhere near Damon's castle? Straining for a better view, she overexerted herself, the blood rushed from her head, her vision blackened, and she fainted back against the pillow.

Violet awoke from her swoon with a knock at the door. "Who's there?" she feebly muttered.

"It's Emma, Milady," a familiar servant's voice rang. "A mendicant now stands upon our stoop! Should I send him away at once?"

"What does he want?" Violet said with a groan, then croaked up a swollen cough.

"I fear he means to preach or teach! He has *a book* in his pocket," Emma said, her voice full of alarm. "Though, while he's here, he may know of a sorcerer's herb that could cure you."

Damon would never admit into his presence a man of the cloth. Yet Damon wasn't home, was he? Violet chuckled beneath her breath, though it hurt her throat, and her pale lips curled into a grin. "Bid him enter and come up and see me. I'd like to speak with him."

"Of course, Milady," Emma said, then shuffled away.

Minutes later, Violet heard voices on the stairs. Then a knock sounded. Knowing it must be the friar, Violet simply said, "Come in."

The door slid open, and in strode the friar. As his gaze fell on her, sick as she was, his brows rose, but his face betrayed no unusual surprise. Likely, he had attended the sick before as plague was not uncommon in the kingdom and mendicants sometimes troubled themselves with the ill.

"Hello. I'm Friar Giles from yonder abbey. And you must be Prince Damon's new . . . wife?" He bowed his head slightly in homage.

"Pull that chair up by the bed," Violet said, pointing weakly. "You must be tired from your wanderings."

Friar Giles grabbed the chair. "Thank you," he said, taking a seat. "I wasn't expecting to be received here. None of the brothers ever have been, if you'll pardon me for saying." Friar Giles wiped the beaded moisture from his brow, seeming apprehensive. "Now, what can I do for you, my dear? You did wish to see me."

Violet felt so hollow, she wondered if she could even speak. "I don't know what I did, but nothing ever turns out right for me, no matter how hard I try. The idea of marrying a prince sounds so wonderful, but I've never been more miserable in all my life. Why must I be so sick? Why must my lord be so . . . devilish and grizzly? Why has this ill luck befallen me?"

Deeply contemplating, Friar Giles peered up at the vaulted ceiling, strewn with cobwebs. Then he leaned forward and clasped her flushed hand. "Tell me, my dear, when did your misfortune first befall you."

"It's a long story," Violet said. "My mother died giving birth to my sister and me. I was raised by my father, a good man, a woodcutter, who always loved us, though I often exasperated him, so he'd speak of me as his 'contrary' child."

"Oh dear," Friar Giles said. "We can't have that!"

Violet groaned in momentary arrest then continued. "To make a long story short, not long ago, I ventured into the forbidden forest with my sister, Daisy. My idea, yes, I admit. There, I stepped in—would you believe it—goblin dung! And you know what happens when you step in goblin dung." Violet peered his way.

"I've heard it's worse bad luck than breaking a mirror." Friar Giles pursed his lips.

Violet nodded weakly then began to cry. "Why me? That's all I want to know. Why, if there's a God, and he loves me, must I suffer so?"

Friar Giles scratched his head. "Why? Oh dear, I must consider how best to answer that question." He pinched his chin, pondering.

"There must be a reason! Now tell me!" Violet said, flashes of anger heating her voice. "I want to know! I demand to know!"

Friar Giles lifted a finger as if to poke a hole of light through a dark ceiling of clouds. "In love, God created Adam and Eve and gave them a beautiful paradise, full of flowers, fruits, and wonders. But they disobeyed, our forebears did, and there are always consequences for disobedience."

"When I trespassed into the forbidden forest," Violet said, "I disobeyed my father."

"You did?" Friar Giles leaned forward at the confession. "When Adam and Eve disobeyed, they accepted a curse."

"And I'm now cursed from goblin dung," Violet said, staring down at her right foot that always seemed so dirty no matter how often she washed it.

"The curse from Adam and Eve's disobedience is called Original Sin. Every person is guilty of it, including you and me. No person can ever be thought of as sin-free."

"Is that why there's so much suffering, sickness, and death?" Violet huffed. "Then what hope is there? What's the cure?"

"The cure?" Friar Giles ran his fingers across his sweated baldness, contemplating the complex question. "Might it be reciting ten Hail Marys?" he wondered aloud. "No, not exactly." He strained in thought. Then his finger shot up. "Prayers to Saint Bernard of Clairvaux! No, wait." He counted on his fingers. "That's not quite right either." He wiped his sweated palms across his tunic. "Relics and penance?" He considered then shook his head. "No, that's not the answer either." He muttered to himself, eyes roving about the room, fruitlessly agonizing. He knew he couldn't recommend hair shirts or flagellation. Her flesh was already too mortified. "Oh dear, it will come to me eventually, yes, just give me time." Friar Giles removed his prayer book, flipping through the pages, searching, then snapping the book shut and repocketing it.

"If you don't know the answer," Violet said, "I'm going to die!"

"I've got it!" Friar Giles' eyes lit up, and a smile spread across his chubby face. "Now I remember!"

"Tell me!" Violet said.

Friar Giles was beaming. "There is one, even Christ Jesus, who can speak to thy condition!"

"Jesus Christ?" Violet gasped. "Now, I remember!"

"Yes, my dear, only the blood of Christ can save you."

"Oh, I've been so foolish, so foolish! Oh, brother, will you pray with me?"

"Certainly, my dear," Friar Giles said. "There is mercy, forgiveness, and grace for all who call upon The Lord." He reached out, again, for her hand. "Let me bless you."

Chapter 10

The Empty Wine Bottle

Rumors grew of trouble on Damon's side of the realm and of Violet's illness. News soon reached the ears of Prince Justin, who grew concerned about his beloved's sister. He wondered what his brother Damon was up to.

One morning, when the sun was shining and the falcons soaring, Justin said to his new bride, "My dearest Daisy, let's go on an outing across country and visit my brother, Damon, and your sister, Violet. They'll be glad to see us."

"What a wonderful idea, an excursion!" Daisy clasped her hands together.

That same day, they set out in a golden carriage. They stopped but once for Justin to pick a red rose to tuck behind Daisy's sun-kissed ear.

Daisy hugged the picnic basket to her breast. "We've brought fine cheeses, fresh scones, and sweet wine. We shall have such a delightful picnic with Violet and Damon." Snug and dandified, she nestled against Justin as the carriage rolled away. "We must bring Violet back for a visit, and Damon can come too."

"Won't that be divine!" Justin had to agree with his mistress mine.

But when they arrived at Damon's castle, the sight of the blood-stained structure was so frightful, it smote Daisy's heart. "I didn't know Violet was staying in such a dreadful place. Where are the flowerbeds and good cheer?"

Violet's screams sounded from a window. That was enough for Prince Justin. "Stay here, My Love, while I investigate this matter."

Justin rushed toward the castle entrance. The guards, recognizing him, allowed him inside. He ran up the stairs to Damon's bedchamber and rapped on the door.

"Who's there?" came Damon's drunken reply.

"Let me in this instant! I've come to see Violet!"

"Go away," Damon's voice slurred from behind the door. "Violet is ill. She's not yours to see, and we don't need your inconveniences today."

When Justin heard his brother's curt dismissal, he beat against the oaken beams even harder. "I demand you let me see her! Open this door at once!"

"I recognize that voice. Justin!" Damon scoffed with lack of appreciation. "There'll be no peace until you get your way. Wait a moment while I make myself decent."

The door finally opened. There stood Damon, chest naked, face stubbly, eyes bloodshot, the top button of his leather pants unfastened. He clutched a dagger in one hand. "Why do you molest our solitude?"

Violet screamed in a sudden seizure. Damon lunged back into the room to attend her, and Justin followed behind him.

The room was in shambles. The drapes were torn. Empty wine bottles cluttered the floor. A painting of some long-forgotten cavalier hung crookedly on the wall. Violet lay wilted on the bed. And blood stained everything, testifying to some ghastly deed.

Justin faced Damon. "You're not the brother I thought you were. Now I take you for a villain, not worthy of a kingdom!"

"You dare insult me?" Damon lurched forward, knife raised. But Justin darted to the side as sprightly as a hart, and Damon crashed into a table.

Violet giggled, peering up from the covers. Damon picked up a dusty vase and threw it at his brother. But Justin promptly ducked, letting the heirloom shatter against the stone wall. Violet laughed again.

"That the best you can do?" Justin asked, balanced on his feet, nimble, and attentive to his brother's moves.

"You're making a fool of me in front of Violet!" Damon growled. "I'll kill you!" Knife in hand, he sprang toward Justin with eyes of fire but stepped on an empty wine bottle that sent him rolling. He crashed to the floor, falling over his own blade. The dirk sunk deeply into his naked chest, piercing his heart. He yowled in pain. He thrashed and twitched on the floor like a fish out of water. Then he lay lifeless and still.

"Damon, you fool!" Justin said, horrified and saddened. "Oh, my brother!"

Violet began to cry. "Damon is dead! Damon is dead!"

"I know. I'm so sorry. He was my brother. What a tragedy!"

"Take me away from here. I want to see Daisy."

"She's outside in the carriage. She wants to see you." Justin moved to the bed to stroke her trembling hand. "I'll take you to her." He picked Violet up and carried her downstairs and out into the sunshine.

When Daisy saw her sister, she fell upon her with many hugs and kisses. "I've missed you, Violet, and you're not at all well. Come home with us, and we'll nurse you back to health and vigor."

Chapter 11

A New Beginning

Justin, Daisy, and Violet returned to Prince Justin's castle. There, Justin placed Violet on a feather bed, with satin sheets and pillows, in a room overlooking a rose garden.

Winter passed, and spring came. Violet's hair regained its luster. She dimpled and blushed with new zest for life, and her eyes sparkled. Soon, she grew well enough to wander about the gardens, which she did every day to smell the flowers, busy with bees, and feel the sun upon her face and shoulders.

Violet and Daisy began taking walks in the fields and forest around the castle. It reminded them of their days with their father, though he had passed away.

One day, while Violet was strolling alone beside a rock wall covered in fragrant honeysuckle, a nobleman, Lord Alfonso, spotted her. He'd never seen such a beautiful sight. With the wind in her dark braids and rippling her white gown, decorated with rose blossoms, Violet seemed the loveliest vision he'd ever beheld, more magical than a unicorn.

For days, Lord Alfonso beseeched Justin for permission to court Violet but to no avail. At last, when Lord Alfonso seemed downright miserable, Justin grew convinced of his honor and allowed him to meet her in the rose garden.

Among the roses, Lord Alfonso fell on his knees before Violet. He slipped a diamond ring over her finger. He pledged to her his undying love and devotion. She gazed into his hazel eyes and understood his pledge was genuine. She felt reborn in mind and spirit. Her disappointments melted like butter in the sun. The last drops of her sickness finally left her, and she became completely whole again.

In the years that followed, the kingdom enjoyed unusual peace and prosperity. The cows produced more milk than the people could even drink. The chickens lay more eggs than the people could even eat. Vineyards thrived with fattened grapes. And every mendicant was received with charity as curses broke with cleansing prayers. For no curse, no foe, no evil, or woe is stronger than the power of prayer. And no greater love has God bestowed than Jesus Christ, so may our praises flow!

When the old king died, he left his whole kingdom to Justin, who ruled the people fairly, as he'd promised, and everyone lived happily and ever after.

Chapter 12

A Clever Eunuch

Gareb peered across the room at Perqueena, curled up on the bed, eyes closed, tawny ringlets matted against the pillow, maroon lipstick smeared across one cheek. Music and laughter drifted from the castle's lower levels. A single candle fizzled on the vanity. A cool breeze gushed through the windows, causing the flame to dance and stirring the canopy bed's curtain.

Gareb eased his stiff buttocks off the stool, wincing at the crick in his back. He crept to Perqueena's bed, his large feet quiet as mice. He lifted a fur up to her waist, clenching his teeth with the task, hoping not to wake her, the situation as precarious as a house of cards that could all come tumbling down in an instant with the fluttering of one eyelid, caked with childish blue make-up.

Gareb sighed to himself. *Maybe I'll get some sleep after all.* He longed for his meager cot like a starving dreg bread, eyeing the cracked doorway leading into the servant's room where he slept.

Perched on his toes like a plump ballerina, he inched across the floor toward his room. He turned back just once to survey the princess. She hadn't stirred. *Sleeping like a baby!* He laughed silently. *Gareb you son of a dandy! You did it!*

He entered his room and quietly closed the door behind him. He hadn't a candle with him, but the full moon shone brightly through the open window onto his ragged mattress. Far off in the nearby woods, a wolf howled.

Gareb yawned. He hadn't been to bed this early in . . . he couldn't remember how long. He approached his cot and settled his tired frame to horizontal with a creak. *This is good.* He yawned again. *Rest, sweet rest, and today I really earned it, for now my story has exposed Perqueena to all the values— justice, perseverance, love, and peace—all the time-honored and transformative principles of political science—that will nourish her budding character into the fine young lady she is destined to become . . . hopefully*, he chuckled skeptically, and with that, drifted into dreams . . .

Boom! Clatter! Bang! Crash! Gareb awoke, heart thudding. He rose from bed and peered into Perqueena's bedchamber. Gone! He ran into the hallway. He turned left then right. At the corridor's end, at the bottom of the first flight of stairs, he found her, lying in a heap.

"Your Majesty!" His mouth dropped open. Perqueena looked like she'd been thrown out with the garbage. Trying to sneak downstairs, she'd tripped over two bags of trash, left in the hallway by the chambermaids, and had fallen down the stone steps, landing atop several bundles of dirty laundry. She lay in litter: half-eaten pears and peach pits, crumpled and burnt parchments, hair clippings, dirty baby diapers— open and leaking their contents—and other bits of refuse. Her dress was torn, silvery threads trailing off the ripped seam like spider webs.

She groaned, wiping her hands on her gown. "Yuk! Rubbish!" Unwelcome smells wafted into Gareb's senses: sour milk, moldy bread, rotting pork pie, and excrement.

Voices sounded down the corridor. A door creaked open, and King Gregar emerged with a lantern. He hastened to the banister. "Perqueena!"

"Puppa, help! I've slipped and fallen!"

"What are you doing down there?" His grayish brown beard bristled above his flannel nightshirt.

"Why aren't you at the ball, Puppa?" Perqueena asked, a hint of fright in her voice.

"Your mother and I retired early, feeling fatigued. Were you sneaking down to the ballroom?" He pressed his lips together, his expression sober. "You were expressly forbidden. Your mother and I told you that you are too young to attend such functions."

Perqueena's mother, barefoot and in her nightgown, appeared at the banister. She held Perqueena's baby brother in her arms, rocking him against her chest. "Perqueena, you didn't!" she spoke in hushed tones as if her daughter's disobedience were unspeakable.

"Gareb, help me back upstairs!" Perqueena whined, lifting her arms like a little child.

Swallowing his laughter, Gareb hurried down the steps to the rescue. "Her Highness should have told *me* to fetch you that glass of water. No matter that I was sleeping. You shouldn't hesitate to send me. I'm ever at your call." Gareb grinned inside, certain he'd win Perqueena's graces with a cover-up.

"Cup of water? Was that all you were up to?" King Gregar's brow rose.

"Yes, Puppa." She nestled into Gareb's arms.

"Why were you sleeping in an evening gown, diamond necklace, and clutch?" Her mother's eyes narrowed with suspicion.

"Tell Mumma why, Gareb."

At the top of the staircase, Gareb set Perqueena on her feet. Immediately, she fled into her bedchamber.

"Her Majesty wanted to show me how she plans to dress for the ball when that grand day arrives." Gareb hunched forward with cringing humility. "Then, poor child, she fell asleep before she could become more properly attired. I didn't wish to wake her."

King Gregar shook his head with a smile. "Perqueena really keeps you hustling, Gareb. I ought to increase your wages."

"Me? Mine?" Gareb pointed to his chest. "I hardly deserve my trifle now." He bowed his head, jaws clenched.

"Really, it's time for a raise, and a vacation. Remind me to speak with you of such things in the future. Now I'd like to get back to rest." He rubbed a tired eye. "I've a grueling schedule tomorrow."

Gareb bowed his head even further, so low it seemed he planned to touch his toes, so low it hid his grin. "I'm ever at your service, Your Highness." He laughed to himself, glad he wasn't headed for the mines.